Books by Natalie Babbitt

Dick Foote and the Shark
Phoebe's Revolt
The Search for Delicious
Kneeknock Rise
The Something
Goody Hall
The Devil's Storybook
Tuck Everlasting
The Eyes of the Amaryllis
Herbert Rowbarge
The Devil's Other Storybook
Nellie: A Cat on Her Own
Bub, or The Very Best Thing
Ouch!
Elsie Times Eight

THE EYES
OF THE
AMARYLLIS

THE EYES
OF THE
AMARYLLIS

NATALIE
BABBITT

SQUARE
FISH

Farrar Straus Giroux
New York

**SQUARE
FISH**

An Imprint of Holtzbrinck Publishers

Square Fish and the Square Fish logo are trademarks of Macmillan and are used by Farrar Straus Giroux under license from Macmillan.

Library of Congress Cataloging-in-Publication Data Available
Library of Congress Catalog Card Number: 77-11862

ISBN 978-0-312-37008-4

Originally published in the United States by Farrar Straus Giroux
First Square Fish Edition: September 2007
10 9 8 7 6 5 4 3 2
mackids.com
AR: 5.0 / F&P: V / LEXILE: 840L

Many waters cannot quench love,

neither can the floods drown it.

Song of Solomon 8:7

THE EYES
OF THE
AMARYLLIS

SEWARD'S WARNING

Listen, all you people lying lazy on the beach, is this what you imagine is the meaning of the sea? Oh, yes, it winks and sparkles as it sways beside you, spreading lacy foam along the sand, as dainty as a handkerchief. But can you really think that this is all it means? The foam, and these tender cowrie shells as pearly as a baby's toes? This purple featherweed floating up fine as the plume of an ostrich? That child in yellow, her face so grave beneath the brim of her linen hat? She sits there filling her bright tin bucket with those tiny shovelsful of sand, as cautious as a pharmacist measuring a dose, and watching her, you murmur to each other, "Sweet! How sweet!"

But listen. That is not the meaning of the sea. Less than a hundred and fifty years ago, on this very spot, out there where that row of rocky points thrusts up above the swells, a ship was lost. There, see? Where those herring gulls are wheeling down? It all looks much the same today: the rocks, and this beach that narrows to a pathway when the tide is in. But on that day at summer's end, the sky went dark, like twilight, with a shrieking wind, and the sea rose up tall as trees. Out there, where the gulls sit sunning now, it flung a ship against the rocks and swallowed her. It swallowed her whole, and every member of her crew. Captain, cargo, every inch of sail and rigging, gone in a single gulp, while the captain's wife stood helpless, watching. Up there, on that little bluff, that's where she stood, shrieking back at the wind, her son gone dumb with horror at her side. And there was nothing to bury afterwards. Nothing. The sea had taken it all, and gave back not one plank or shred of canvas.

That is part of the meaning. But there's more. A little later, three months or four, a young man broke his heart over a foolish girl. Nothing to remark about in that, you think. But he was an artist, that young man. He had carved a figurehead for the Amaryllis, the ship that was swallowed, carved it in the likeness of the captain's wife—proud and handsome, with long red hair. Then he up and broke his heart over a foolish

· 4 ·

girl, and one morning very early, while the mist was still thick, he climbed into a dinghy and rowed himself straight out, out there well past the place where that sailboat skims along. He rowed out early in the morning, and he vanished. Oh, they found the dinghy later, just here, washed up, its oars stowed neat and dry inside. But he was not washed up, though they searched the shore for days. He was swallowed, they said at last, swallowed like the Amaryllis.

But he was not quite swallowed. Listen. That is the rest of the meaning of the sea. You lie here so unthinking—have you forgotten that the surface of the earth is three-fourths water? Those gulls out there, they know it better than you. The sea can swallow ships, and it can spit out whales upon the beach like watermelon seeds. It will take what it wants, and it will keep what it has taken, and you may not take away from it what it does not wish to give. Listen. No matter how old you grow or how important on the land, no matter how powerful or beautiful or rich, the sea does not care a straw for you. That frail grip you keep on the wisp of life that holds you upright—the sea can turn it loose in an instant. For life came first from the sea and can be taken back. Listen. Your bodies, they are three-fourths water, like the surface of the earth.

Ashes to ashes, the Bible says, and maybe so—but the ashes float on the water of you, like that purple featherweed floating on the tide. Even your tears are salt.

You do not listen. What if I told you that I was that carver of figureheads, the one they said was swallowed by the sea? The breeze in your ears, it carries my voice. But you only stretch on your fluffy towels and talk of present things, taking the sea for granted. So much the worse for you, then. My two Genevas listened, long ago, and understood.

"Well, Mother," said the big man uneasily, turning his hat round and round in his hands.

"Well, George," the old woman returned. Her voice was strong and brisk, but, for him, a little critical. She looked up at him from her wing chair by the sunny window and saw—her son, yes, but also a stranger, well into middle age, tall but stooped, with the pale skin and scratchy-looking clothes of an inland man of business. And she saw in him also what he had been: a happy, wild-haired boy running barefoot on the beach. The two were one and the same, no doubt, but she loved the man because she had loved the boy. For her, the boy had been much easier to love.

"So you've broken your ankle," the man said.

"So it seems," she answered. She looked down impatiently at her foot propped up on a hassock. It was thick with bandages and wooden splints, and beside it on the floor a crutch lay waiting. "It's a nuisance, but there you are. Where's my granddaughter? Where's my namesake?"

"She's out on the beach. She's—well, she's never seen the sea before, you know. I suppose she's . . . interested in having a look."

"Interested! Yes, I should imagine so." The old woman smiled faintly.

The man took a deep breath. "Look here, Mother, you know we've always wanted you to come and live with us in Springfield. Now that you're laid up and can't take care of yourself, it's a good time to leave this godforsaken place and come inland where we can look after you."

The old woman shook her head. "It's good of you, George, of course. But when I wrote to you, that wasn't what I had in mind at all. You've brought Geneva down to stay with me, haven't you? That was the plan, wasn't it? My ankle will mend, and when it does, I'll go on the same as I always have."

"I just don't understand it," her son exploded then. "All by yourself here, year after year! The sea pounding, day and night, the dampness, this blasted sand everywhere. And the wind! It never stops! I can hardly bear it for five minutes, and you've been listening to it for thirty years!"

"Fifty, George. You've forgotten. Your father and I, we came here fifty years ago."

"No, but I meant . . ."

"I know what you meant," she said. "You're thinking it's thirty years since the day your father was drowned."

The man gripped his hat more firmly. "All right, Mother, never mind that. Be sensible for once and come back with me. There's plenty of room for three in the buggy, and we can send a wagon later for your things. Surely you can't be so all-fired stubborn about it now, when you can scarcely hobble."

His mother shook her head again. "I don't need you, George. Not yet. It's not time yet. I'll come to you at Christmas, just as I've always done. But the rest of the year I belong right here. Geneva can take care of me till my ankle mends, and then you can come and fetch her."

"But, Mother!"

The old woman frowned at him and her eyes flashed. "George! Enough! We've had this argument a hundred times, and it bores me. You ran away from here a long time ago, and that's all right for you. But I will not budge an inch, not one inch, until . . ." She paused and looked away. Her anger seemed to leave her all at once, and she sighed. "George. Send Geneva in to me and then—go away, George. We only make each other cross."

At this the man seemed to sag a little. A look of pain crossed his face, and he turned half away from her, toward the door, though he watched her still. She was as handsome and vigorous as ever, her gray hair still streaked with red, her back straight as . . . a mast, he thought unwillingly, and then corrected it. Straight as a yardstick. A safer image.

She saw that he was watching her, and her face softened. "George. Dear boy, come and kiss me."

He went to her at once and knelt, and she put her arms around him and pulled him close. For a moment, the last long thirty years dissolved. They were mother and child again, she newly widowed, he newly father-less, and they clung to each other. Then she loosened her hold and pushed him away gently. "Tell me," she said, smiling at him. "Geneva—what sort of child is she getting to be, do you think?"

"She's exactly like you," he said, sitting back on his heels.

The first Geneva Reade nodded and her eyes twinkled. "It's a judgment on you, George. Well, send her in. And then go home to Springfield and leave me in peace."

The big man kissed his mother's cheek and stood up, putting on his hat. Then, at the door, he said carefully, "I should have thought, though, that you'd want to come away from this spot. I couldn't stand it, looking out there every day, remembering. I'd have gone mad by now."

"Mad?" said his mother. "Well, perhaps I am a little mad."

"Mother," he blurted then, turning back to her, "for the love of heaven, watch out for Jenny. She's all we've got. Don't let her—"

"Hang your clothes on a hickory limb, and don't go near the water," the old woman chanted, bobbing her head from side to side. And then she said, scornfully, "Don't worry. I'll keep her out of the sea. You weren't such a faintheart before your father died."

The man's face closed. "I'll be back in three weeks," he told her flatly. "To fetch Jenny home. And if you're not mended by then, you'll come and stay with us till you are, whether you want to or not."

"Goodbye, George," said his mother, dismissing

him. "Have a pleasant ride home. We'll see you in a month or two."

"Three weeks, Mother. Not a moment longer."

"*Goodbye*, George," said the first Geneva Reade.

The journey that takes a traveler from inland places to the sea will follow roads that stay, in themselves, exactly the same, but they seem to change entirely. Carefree and busy, now leaf-shadowed, now blank and blinding in the summer sunshine, they stretch ahead importantly between green fields, and the air lies lightly on them. But by the time they have come within three miles, then two, then one, of their destination, they have turned submissive. The trees stand back and stand thin, and scrub pines appear, ragged as molting birds. The edges of the roads are lost now in drifts of sand, and the grass, thinner, like the trees, is rough and tall, rising, kneeling, rising, kneeling, as the breeze combs by.

There seems to be more sky here, a great deal more,

so that the traveler is made aware, perhaps for the first time, that he moves along quite unprotected on the crust of the earth and might do well to move with caution, lest all at once he fall off, fall up, endlessly, and disappear. So he holds his gaze to the ground and finds that the air has grown heavy with new, wet smells, and the roads and everything around them look uncared-for. But this is not the case. They are cared for with the closest attention—by the sea.

The second Geneva Reade had observed all this on the way to Gran's house and was astonished by it in spite of the heavy presence beside her in the buggy. Her father had not spoken a word for miles, and he had allowed the horse to slow its pace to a clopping walk. His clenched hands, wrapped in the reins, were white at the knuckles. Jenny observed this, also, but she could not worry about it now. She was going to see the ocean for the first time in her life.

To be away from home—to stay with Gran and help her while her ankle mended—this seemed a very grownup thing to do, and Jenny had boasted about it to her friends. But in truth she was a little alarmed about that part, though her grandmother, whom she had seen before only for the two weeks of the yearly Christmas season, had long been a figure of romance to her. Gran was not like other grandmothers, smelling of starch or mothballs, depending on the time of year, and spending their time watering their plants. Gran stood straight and proud. Her face and arms were sunburned. And though she talked and listened, there always seemed to be something else on her mind, something far more absorbing than Christmas conversation.

But Jenny did not care for household chores, and was not at all sure that somewhere in her lay hidden the makings of a bedside nurse. So it wasn't that part of her adventure that excited her. No, the real enticement was the ocean. But this she could not admit. She was the only one of her friends who had never been to the shore. Preposterous, when it was only thirty miles from Springfield! But her father had never let her come, had always refused to discuss it. He hardly ever went, himself, to see Gran at her house.

But now, because of Gran's ankle, all that had changed. She was going to see the ocean, and she had all she could do to keep from bouncing on the buggy's padded seat. When would the water show itself? Over the next rise? Now! The buggy started up—and then she had gasped once and sat erect and very still.

For there it was, suddenly, the great Atlantic, so

vast a thing that all of her imaginings could never have prepared her. It stretched away so far beyond the grassy plain that its sharp horizon curved to prove the roundness of the planet. In an instant she felt diminished, and with that new sensation came an unexpected sense of freedom. The breath she had caught and held slipped out in a long sigh, and she turned her head to see how her father was responding to the sight. But his face was rigid as a stone.

So she had turned back, and as the buggy rolled nearer, the coastline below them revealed itself slowly. A bay emerged and, far to the leftward tilt of its concavity, a tidy-looking town, with docks and the hulls of a few small ships. Then, as the buggy, reaching a fork, turned right, she saw that there were houses scattered all along the shore. Far to the right, however, they sat fewer and farther between until at last there was only one house, quite by itself, on a low bluff at the farthest edge of the bay, where the land curved slowly in and down and sank a heavy arm into the water.

"Is that Gran's house?" she had asked, pointing.

"Yes," said her father.

"That's where you lived when you were little?"

"Yes," he said shortly.

Her head filled at once with a thousand questions, but it was clear that he didn't want to talk. "I can ask Gran," she had thought to herself. "Later."

When the buggy rolled down and stopped at last beside the house, Jenny had climbed out slowly, her eyes turned to the beach. "Can I go and look?" she pleaded. "Before I go in to see Gran?"

"All right, I guess so," her father said. "But, Jenny, remember what I told you. Stay back from the water. Don't ever forget that it's dangerous." And then, taking down her satchel, he had gone to the door of the house, knocked once, and stepped inside.

The sea did not look dangerous. Jenny saw the whole of its low-tide shore behavior in one long glance —how it tipped and slopped, sifting the wet sand, stroking the beach with sliding foam. Well up on this beach, a straggling fringe of seaweed, like a scratchy penline, lay drying where the last high tide had stranded it, and here, too, intermingled, had been left abandoned pebbles by the million and broken bits of shell. Above the seaweed the toast-colored sand was loose and warm, and she longed to take off her shoes and stockings and dig her toes into it. Not now. Later. After her father had gone. Gran had promised her that if she, Jenny, were ever allowed to visit here, there would be much to do on the beach, things that could only be done correctly if one were barefoot.

Jenny took a cautious step over the seaweed line, down to where the sand was hard and wet, and at once a sly finger of foam slid up and curled around her ankle. She leapt back and the foam slipped away with a sigh, to be lost beneath the curl of the next small wave. Now new fingers of foam reached for her up the sand, and she retreated behind the seaweed reluctantly. Another wave, a soft thump, the slide of foam, repeated over and over again. She watched it, amazed and faintly hypnotized, and the feeling of freedom that had come to her at first grew deeper. Wisps of her dark red hair, tied back so neatly at home by her mother, blew about her face as the breeze swept past her, and suddenly it seemed as if she could hear it speaking. *True to yo-o-o-ou*, it whispered, and the foam answered: *Yes-s-s* (thump) *yes-s-s* (thump) *yes-s-s.*

"Jenny!"

She heard her father's voice behind her and, turning, plodded up across the sand to where he stood at the edge of the swaying grass.

"Jenny, look at you. You've soaked one foot already," he said despairingly. "Will you promise to stay safe, now? Will you be careful? I've kept you away from this place as long as I could, and—I know you're nearly grown, but still, it worries me to death to leave you here."

"I'll be careful, Papa," she said.

He put his hands on her shoulders and peered into her face, and then, dropping his hands, he shrugged. "Well, do your best to be useful to your grandmother. It's remarkable how she never seems to change, but still, she's getting on. You'll see. She's waiting for you —better go on in. I'll be back in three weeks."

"All right, Papa."

He left her, then, and climbed into the buggy, and as he urged the horse into a turn, she saw the stiffness of his shoulders ease, and he looked back at her almost cheerfully. "Goodbye!" he called.

She answered, "Goodbye," and added, to herself, "He's happy to be leaving." She watched him go and felt stranded and lonely, like the pebbles, but then she turned back for one more look at the sea and the lonely feeling fled away. For it seemed as if she had known this beach and loved it all her life, that she belonged here; that coming to this place, with its endless sky and water, was a kind of coming home.

"Quick, child, come and tell me," said Gran from her chair when Jenny went inside. "What did you find on the beach? Anything unusual?" And then she caught herself. "Dear me, listen to the old lady, ranting on without even saying hello." She held out her arms and Jenny went to her and gave her a hug of greeting.

"Well!" said Gran. "So here you are at last! Let me look at you." She sat back, folding her arms, and tilted her head solemnly. "Your father says you're just like me, and I know he thinks I'm stubborn and unreasonable. Are you?"

"I don't know," said Jenny, laughing. "I guess so, sometimes."

"You've still got my red hair," Gran observed, "but otherwise you've changed a little since Christmas. How old are you now?"

"Eleven," said Jenny. "Last February."

"Yes, and now it's the middle of August," said Gran. "So you're halfway to twelve. Not a child at all, really, though you mustn't expect me to stop calling you a child. I have a hard time remembering new things, sometimes. But I can remember the old things as if they happened yesterday. I met your grandfather for the first time when I was thirteen. Imagine that! He was twenty-one, and as handsome . . . well, as handsome as a walrus."

"A walrus!" said Jenny, laughing again. "Walruses aren't handsome."

"Well, now, that's a matter of taste," said Gran with a smile. "Your grandfather was a big man, heavyset, with a fine, big pair of mustaches. To me he was wonderfully handsome, and I fell in love with him at once."

"When you were thirteen?"

"Yes, indeed."

"I'm not in love with anyone," said Jenny, "and no one's in love with me."

"Someone will be, someday," said Gran.

"Oh, no," said Jenny. "I don't expect it. I'm much too ugly."

"Ugly!" Gran exclaimed, throwing up a hand in mock dismay. "But, child, how can you be ugly when you look so much like me? Your grandfather fell in love with me, remember."

"When you were thirteen?"

"Oh, no, certainly not," said Gran. "Years later. He was a sailor—well, you know that, of course—and when he wasn't on a voyage he would come to Springfield to visit his sister. Your Great-aunt Jane. It was ten years later, when I was twenty-three and he was thirty-one—that's when he noticed me. Two years after that he had his own ship, and we were married and came to live right here, in this house." She looked about her with satisfaction at the tidy, low-ceilinged room with its simple chairs and tables, and its mantel full of odd bits of china. "Then—let's see. Your father was born six years after that, in the spring of '36, and then when he was fourteen, that's when the *Amaryllis* was . . . lost. Out there on the rocks in a terrible storm." She said this calmly enough, tipping her head to indicate the stretch of sea outside the window behind her, but a look of intensity came to her face and she leaned forward and put a hand on

Jenny's arm. "You went down to the beach just now?"

"Yes," said Jenny.

"Did you see anything? Anything at all?"

"Well," said Jenny, "I saw sand, and pebbles, and some long, stringy-looking weeds, and—the ocean, Gran! Oh, it's wonderful! It makes me feel . . ."

"Free!" said Gran triumphantly.

"Yes, that's it exactly," said Jenny, surprised. "How did you know?"

"How did I know?" said Gran. "What a question! It keeps me strong, that sense of freedom. And yet your father doesn't seem to feel it at all. Isn't that peculiar! But, child, was there nothing unusual on the beach? Nothing washed up?"

"What sort of thing?" asked Jenny, puzzled by the urgency in her grandmother's voice. "What are you looking for?"

"Never mind," said Gran, turning away from it. "Plenty of time for that later. Hand me the almanac on that table over there. I'll check the tides and then we'll have supper. Yes. Thank you, my dear. Now, let me see . . . here we are." She ran a fingertip down the page. "I thought so. High tide at 12:15 tonight. Good. Well! Now for supper."

"What shall I cook?" asked Jenny nervously. This was the part she had dreaded.

But Gran said, mercifully, "Cook? Why, nothing at all! What an idea!" She bent and picked up the crutch, and then, pulling herself up onto her good leg, she stood tall and straight and glared at her granddaughter. "I'm not an invalid, you know. And I don't intend to sit here and be fussed over. I shall do the cooking."

"But, Gran, I thought—"

"Never mind what you thought. Follow me. You can set the table, and fetch and carry now and then, but that's not why I sent for you."

Jenny tried hard to disguise her relief, but Gran, looking at her narrowly, recognized it anyway. "You don't like to cook?"

"No," said Jenny. "Not very much."

"Neither do I," said Gran. "We shall do as little of it as we possibly can without starving. Come along."

In the dining room, over the mantel, hung a drawing of a ship. "That's the *Amaryllis*," said Gran as they sat down to eat. "A brig, she was, a big two-master. A beautiful thing to see. Your grandfather owned her, and he was her captain, too. He sailed her up and down the coast from Maine to the Caribbean."

"Did you ever go along?" asked Jenny.

"No, I never did. Women aren't welcome on trading ships, you know, and anyway, I had your father to care for. No, I stayed right here. And yet in a way I did go along. Look more closely there. Do you see the figurehead? Go and look."

Jenny got up from her chair and went to peer at the picture. "It's a woman," she reported, "and she's holding some kind of flower in her hands."

"It's a likeness of me," said Gran proudly. "That's an amaryllis I'm holding. A big red lily from the islands. Your grandfather thought they were very handsome, and he always said they reminded him of me. A romantic notion, but that's the way he was. So he named the ship after them, and put me on the prow. He tried time and again to bring me one—an amaryllis —but they always died on the way. Sometimes he'd be gone for months at a time, you see. It's a long way down to the islands."

"You couldn't have had much time with him," said Jenny, coming back to the table. "If he was gone so much. Weren't you lonely?"

"One gets used to it," said Gran. "But when the *Amaryllis* was due, I would go out to the bluff there and watch for it, and then we'd have such lovely parties when he was home again."

"My father comes home at the same time every day," said Jenny. "Five-thirty, when he's closed up the store."

"I know," said Gran, without interest. "It sounds very dull."

Jenny thought so, too, now. It seemed unbearably dull. But she added, in unconscious imitation, "Still, one gets used to it."

"I suppose so," said Gran.

Supper was nearly over when suddenly Gran put down her fork. She lifted her head, holding out a hand in a signal for silence. "Shh!" she whispered. "There! Do you hear it?"

Jenny listened. Nothing came to her ears but the breeze and the slap of waves. She looked at Gran questioningly. "What? What should I hear?"

"The tide," said Gran. "It's turned." She stared at Jenny and her eyes were blank, as if she'd forgotten for an instant that she was not alone. Then she was herself again, but with a difference. Something in her concentration had shifted, some inner curtain dropping while another opened. "Finish your supper," she said. "Then we'll clear away and go out to the beach."

Leaning on her crutch, with Jenny at her other side to steady her, Gran stumped across the swaying grass to the little bluff that thrust out before the house. On three sides of it, the land dropped steeply four feet or so to the beach, so that it formed a small point, and here there was an old wooden bench. Gran eased herself down onto it and settled her bundled ankle out in front of her with a grimace of pain.

"You shouldn't go about on it so much," said Jenny.

"I have a doctor to tell me what to do," said Gran indifferently. "And if I don't pay attention to him, what makes you think I'll pay attention to you? Now, be a good child and sit here beside me. It will be dark soon. We've only an hour before bedtime, and I want to talk to you."

Jenny sat down and waited, but Gran was silent, leaning forward, staring out to sea. The sun, dropping rapidly behind them, seemed to be drawing the daylight with it like a veil, revealing behind the blue, as it slid away, the endlessness of space. A star appeared, and before them the green-brown waves took on an iridescence and spilled a sort of glow along the sand.

"At this time of day," said Gran at last, "it looks different. There almost seems to be a light . . . coming up from the bottom."

Jenny had to lean close to hear her grandmother's words, for the breeze had quickened and was whispering again in her ears. "The wind almost talks, doesn't it?" she said shyly.

Gran, at this, turned and looked at her closely. "So you hear it, too? Good. I was hoping for it. Give me your hand."

Gran's sun-browned hand was dry and strong, hard in spite of the rumpled skin at her wrist and knuckles. But her long fingers, holding Jenny's, were trembling slightly. Jenny looked down and saw how different this hand was from her mother's, so soft and padded and white. "It's important to look after your hands," her mother always said. "A lady doesn't go about with ragged fingernails, dear, and get her skin all chapped.

You must learn to take more care. Your hands look so . . . *used*, Jenny. Like a boy's." Now Jenny saw that her hands were like Gran's, and for the first time she was proud of them. Oh, they were younger, to be sure. But very like.

"Pay close attention, Geneva," said Gran. "There's very little time. We must go to bed soon, and sleep, if we're to be fresh again by midnight."

"Midnight?" Jenny echoed.

"Certainly," said Gran. "We must be up again at midnight."

"But why?"

"High tide, child," said Gran, and then she stiffened. "Hist! Look there."

Jenny, startled, turned her head in the direction of Gran's gaze, and saw the figure of a man trudging slowly toward them along the shadowed beach. It was impossible to see his features, for his head was bowed, but Jenny could tell that he was rather small and hunched. He wore a dark, short coat of some heavy material, and his hands were plunged deep into his pockets. Then, as he came abreast of them, below the little bluff, he halted and looked up, and in the last gleam of daylight, Jenny saw a bearded face, ruined and rutted, with quiet but watchful eyes. "Good evening, Mrs. Reade," he said to Gran, and his voice had the same insistent rustle as the wind.

"Good evening, Seward," said Gran, and her fingers gave Jenny's a brief, unconscious squeeze.

The man stood looking at Gran for a moment, and then his gaze shifted to Jenny and his eyebrows lifted. But he said nothing more, and, dropping his head again, he moved off slowly down the beach, disappearing at last in the gloom.

"Who was that?" asked Jenny.

"Then you saw him, too," said Gran, and there was evident relief in her voice.

"Yes, of course I saw him," said Jenny. "What do you mean? How could I not have seen him?"

"Never mind," said Gran. "Now. There's very little time." Her fingers tightened once more on her granddaughter's. "Geneva, listen carefully. Do you believe in things you can't explain?"

Jenny sat silent, considering. No one had ever asked her such a question before. At last she said, "Like things in fairy tales?"

"No, child," said Gran. "I mean—that all the daily things we do, and all the things we can touch and see in this world, are only one part of what's there, and that there's another world around us all the time that's mostly hidden from us. Do you ever think such things?"

"Well," said Jenny, confused and a little uncomfortable, but pleased, too, that Gran should speak to her this way. "Well, I think so. Yes, sometimes. Especially at night. But it's kind of scary."

"Ah!" said Gran. "Then you don't see quite what I mean. To me it's not 'scary' at all. Why should things we can't explain have to be frightening?"

"I don't know," said Jenny, "but they are. Sometimes, at night, I'm afraid to hang my hand down over the edge of the bed, because . . . well . . ."

"Because you're afraid something will grab it from under the bed!" said Gran, finishing the thought for her. "I know. Everyone has that notion sometimes. But that's our imagination, Geneva. I'm not talking about imagined things. I'm talking about . . . well, never mind. I'll just have to take a chance and hope you'll understand. You did see Seward just now, after all . . ." Her voice trailed off, but before Jenny could speak, she began again. "At high tide, child, I want you to come down here to the beach and search. I've done it by myself for thirty years, and then, last week, I stumbled in the sand and broke my silly ankle, and now, with that and this blasted crutch, I can't get about well enough. Not to do it properly. That's why I sent for you, Geneva. I'm depending on you to help me. You must come and search, and if you find anything, you must bring it back at once. You must get there first, before Seward."

"Seward? The man who just went by?" said Jenny.

"Yes. He goes for miles along the beach," said Gran, "and picks things up."

"But who is he?"

Gran ignored this question. "I'll give you a lantern at midnight. Then you must come out and search."

"But what am I to look for?" Jenny cried. "I don't understand at all."

Gran drew her hand away and laced her own fingers tightly together. There was a long pause, and then: "For thirty years," she said, "I've waited for a sign from my darling. It will come, it *will*, on the high tide someday. Any day now, surely. But someone must be here to find it. You must be my legs now, and my eyes, on the beach. To think of its coming, and my not even seeing it! No, Geneva, you must find it for me."

"A sign? From my grandfather? Oh, Gran!" said Jenny, dumfounded. "Gran, how?"

"When I tell you," said Gran, "you mustn't think

I've gone mad." It was nearly dark, but Jenny could see that her grandmother's eyes burned brightly, her heavy brows drawn down into a furrow. "I've never talked of this to anyone before. But now it appears I must. Dear child, the *Amaryllis*, and all the swallowed ships . . . I know it seems impossible, and yet it's true. Seward told me. At first I didn't believe him, but then, when I saw how things were, I knew. He watches me. He has to, poor soul—he hasn't any choice. And he knows I'm waiting for a sign. Geneva, namesake, after the *Amaryllis* sank, I walked on the beach for weeks. I wanted something back—a button, a length of rope, anything to make the sinking real. Because it was so strange, Geneva, so strange to stand here and watch the ship go down in such a gulp, so near to shore, and then—for there to be nothing! Do you see how strange it was? It was as if there had never been a ship at all, and no beloved husband—as if my happy life with him had only been a dream that was over suddenly and I had waked from it to find that it had never even happened."

"But, Gran," said Jenny, "you had my father, didn't you? Why wasn't he a good reminder?"

"George?" said Gran, surprised. "Yes, yes, there was George. But he was so . . . he didn't make the difference I needed. So I walked on the beach and waited for something, some sign to hold on to. But Nicholas Irving had been drowned, too, at almost the same time, and nothing had been found of him, either. It seemed as if the sea was taking everything, and giving nothing back."

"Who was Nicholas Irving?" Jenny asked.

"Poor Nicholas!" said Gran. "So gifted. He carved the figurehead for the *Amaryllis*, and made that drawing in the dining room. He could do things with a pen or a bit of wood or plaster that were wonderful to see. He drowned himself, they said." Gran's voice turned careful for a moment. "I don't know. That's another story. But, Geneva, some time after that, one night, Seward came to me on the beach, and when he told me—when we walked and talked—he told me things, and at last I understood. And I knew that there *would* be a sign sent back to me and that I must wait and watch for it."

"Then you mean," said Jenny, "that my grandfather's ship is down there somewhere, and that something is bound to be washed ashore sometime?"

"No, Geneva," said Gran, and her eyes burned bright again. "I mean that there will be a *sign*. Not by accident, but on purpose. From him. Because the swallowed ships, it keeps them at the bottom to guard its treasures. And all the drowned sailors are there, Geneva, all the poor drowned sailors, sailing the ships forever at the bottom of the sea."

Upstairs, in the room that had been her father's, Jenny leaned against the big four-poster bed and blinked. She hardly recognized herself against these strange new backgrounds. She had often thought of herself as a character in a story—a story where nothing ever happened. But now it was as if she had been lifted bodily into a new story—Gran's—where everything was different. Out there on the beach, Gran had talked to her as if they were two women, not a grandmother and a child, and Gran expected her to understand.

But what would her father say? He had told her that Gran was getting on. He had said that Jenny would "see." Did he know, then, about this waiting for a sign? No, somehow Jenny knew he didn't. And all at once she feared that, if he were to know, he would decide that Gran *was* mad. He had not wanted Jenny to come here. And he might never have allowed it at all if he had known about the waiting. Would he have come, instead, by himself, and taken Gran away? But taken her where?

There was a building at home, a large, square building of yellow brick, standing in a barren, treeless yard inside an iron fence. There were rows and rows of narrow windows, blank and silent, and some of them were barred. Remembering that building, Jenny shuddered. They had passed it many times, she and her friends, passed it on purpose, taking the long way home from school to scare themselves with what they hoped and feared to see. Or hear. For the building was a madhouse. If her father thought that Gran was mad, would he put her there, behind those silent windows? No, he wouldn't do a thing like that. That was Springfield. Here, things were different.

Then, as she leaned against her father's bed, the music at the back of her thoughts—the music of the rising tide—pushed through and commanded her attention. She went to the window and looked down at the beach. The water was black now, much blacker than the star-strewn sky, and it looked thick, almost solid, like gelatin. But the foam still glowed with an inner light that made it seem a different substance from the spilling waves, like a magic kind of lace on a black satin skirt.

A skirt, with lace. People always talked about the sea as if it were a "she," while Father Neptune was a "he." But the sea was real, and Neptune only a made-up figure, silly, really, with his trident and his curly beard. Silly to think of a trident, a fork—for that was all it was—as a weapon for a ruler of the sea. You couldn't calm those waves, or stir them up, for that matter, with a fork. Gran had called the sea an "it." Yes, that was better. It was far too big to be a he or a she. It was beyond such small distinctions. And it did not have a ruler; it was a rule all by itself.

She opened the window, and the cool, wet breeze rushed in. Behind her, in a sconce above the bureau, the flames of the candles leaned and flickered, so that her shadow shifted. She sighed and, closing the window, wandered over to the washstand. There was a mirror there, with a bone frame and handle, and she picked it up and stared at her reflection. It, at least, looked just the same as always. "I'm ugly," she told herself, studying the heavy brows, too heavy; the narrow nose, too narrow; the pale white skin, too pale, with too many freckles. She had always gone along content with her face. It hadn't seemed important in the least. But lately she had begun to suspect, with sorrow, that a face might be very important. And hers, her face, was ugly. Would always be ugly. There was nothing to be done for it.

"Still, my hair is all right," she allowed herself. "It's the only nice thing about me." She had decided that she would never cut it. Not a single strand. Someday, when she was sixteen, she would be old enough to twist it up, away from her neck, and wear it in a heavy coil on the back of her head. Like her mother. Like Gran. Gran's hair must have looked like this when she was young. There was lots of red in it still. Red was unusual. Special. Like Gran herself.

From somewhere downstairs, a clock chimed ten. Jenny struggled out of her clothes—her rumpled dress, her stockings, her petticoat, her bloomers—and pulled a cotton nightgown over her head. "My father slept in this bed when he was little," she told herself, climbing in, but it was impossible to see him as someone her own size, so she gave it up and snuggled down under the covers. After all, he had always been a man to her, always old, always married to her mother. It was impossible to imagine him young, growing up, falling in love like someone in a play. Of course they loved each other, her father and mother. Of course they did. But they didn't talk about it, as Gran had. Gran had declared, "Your grandfather fell in love with *me*," and later, on the beach, she had said, in a different sort of voice, "For thirty years I've waited for a sign from my darling." My darling! Jenny's father and mother did not call each other "my darling." Jenny lay staring in the candlelight, and all at once decided that she would do anything for Gran. Whatever she was asked to do. And then, with the music of the sea in her ears, she fell asleep.

It seemed as if she'd only dozed a moment before she woke to hear Gran calling her. "Geneva! Get up! High tide." Dazed, she stumbled out of bed, found her shoes, pulled them on without thinking, and shrugged into her dressing gown. Downstairs, Gran waited at the door, a lantern dangling from one hand, the other gripping her crutch. She was still dressed, and Jenny said, "Gran! You haven't been to bed!"

"I slept in my chair here," said Gran, "in the parlor. Come, quickly. You must get down to the beach."

Outside, the noise of the water was deafening, and

Jenny could see in the dimness that the waves were high now, surging forward, tumbling over with a crash that flogged the beach, almost made it quake. The foam spilled up and slid away in a rapid rush of bubbles, spreading nearly to the foot of the little bluff, so that the beach was narrowed to a slender strip of damp, cold sand.

It had been gentle and playful before, this ocean, but now it was dark, magnificent, alarming. Jenny hesitated, apprehensive, but Gran did not seem to notice. Instead, she moved on firmly, out to the wooden bench. "Quick!" she urged, over the roar of the wind and water. "There! Along the tide line! Now, before Seward comes! Search all along the edges of the foam. Anything you find, *anything*, bring it to me at once."

Jenny took the lantern and slid down the bluff to the beach. She paused as the rolling water seized her feet and dragged at them, and for a moment she was filled with dread. But then, in her ears, the wind rose up distinct from the noise of the water. It called to her, and a strange new rising feeling of excitement filled her, driving out the fear. She plunged off through the foam, her shoes a sodden wreck at once, her nightgown and wrapper soaked and plastered to her legs. The lantern, swinging high from her lifted hand, rocked a golden arc of light across the streaming sand, and she forgot to notice how cold the water was, how rasping when it flung its load of broken shell and seaweed round her ankles. She was aware only of freedom and exhilaration. Springfield—what was that? Buggies and school and being careful—what were they? Gran did not say, "Be careful," because Gran was not afraid. Here they were all one thing, she, and Gran, the wild, dark, rushing water, and the wind. Up and back she went along the beach, passing the bluff a dozen times, searching through the fringes of the tide. She wanted now, more than anything else, to believe in the sign and to find it. For Gran.

But there was nothing. And at last, spent and disappointed, she waded back to the bluff and stood below it, shivering now from cold. "There's nothing, Gran. Nothing at all."

"Yes," said Gran. "The tide is turning back. Might as well come in now, and go to bed."

Inside the house, Gran paused and looked at her and Jenny saw that her concentration had shifted back. Gran was her afternoon self, her usual self, again. "Why, bless me, child, you're soaked to the skin! And your shoes—why ever did you wear your shoes? But, of course. You didn't realize—how foolish of me. Go and towel off. Have you another nightgown? Put it on, and I'll go light the fire and make some tea."

Upstairs, Jenny piled her dripping clothes thoughtlessly into the basin on the washstand and rubbed herself dry. And then, warm again, wrapped in the towel, she picked up the bone-handled mirror once more and peered at her face. The pale white skin was rosy now, and the eyes that stared back at her under those heavy brows were shining. "Gran isn't mad," she reassured this new reflection. "She's just—well, she's got the sea in her, somehow. I can feel it, too. Everything feels different here. I'm different. Oh, I wish I could stay forever!"

When Jenny woke up in the morning, she climbed out of bed and went at once to the window. The beaming sea lay far out, at low tide, much as it had the afternoon before, and it sparkled in the early sunshine, flicking tiny, blinding flashes of light into the air. The horizon, impossibly far away, invited her. The soft breeze invited her. This was a mermaid morning—a morning for sitting on the rocks and combing your long red hair. She was enchanted by it, and found that the feeling of freedom was stronger than ever. Why, she had walked on the beach last night, when the sea was up and roaring, and no one had said, "You mustn't." No one had said, "It's dangerous." Imagine! Gran was taking it for granted that she could take care of herself. And all at once she felt stronger here, at the edge of this other world, than she ever had in Springfield.

But what about the *Amaryllis* and the sign? What about the man on the beach? All right. There were things she didn't understand. But this morning they didn't seem to matter. It was enough that Gran understood them. Gran needed her to do the searching now. Well, she would do it. In Springfield, to get up in the middle of the night on such an errand would be outrageous. But this was not Springfield. This was a different place. Gran's place.

And so, as the pattern of her days and nights took hold, Springfield receded to a distant blur. It began to seem that she had always lived here by the sea, had always watched for the turning of the tide. She had come to this house on a Saturday afternoon, and on Sunday she could run as free along the beach as her father had those long, long years before, shoeless, joyful, and at home. These first few days were bright and hot, the sea a wide green smile. She collected little shells and, once, a sturdy clam who lived for a day in a bucket of sand and sea water, spitting occasionally like a miniature geyser, before she put him back.

Each day the tide came in a little later, advancing slowly, so that by Thursday she was out with Gran long after midnight and again late in the afternoon. Sometimes, when the wind was up, the waves were tall, and sometimes they rolled in gently, like breathing, deep and slow. But there was never anything to find, nothing whatever washed up except the seaweed and the outcast pebbles. And soon the search began to seem to her to be a sort of game she played with the sea, she and Gran, twice every day, the way some people play at reading cards for prophecies, caught by belief and disbelief like a pin between two magnets. But believing didn't matter with games, and anyway, by Thursday, the night sky was turning to dawn when the time came for the search, and the high tides of the daylight hours were frothy and warm with sunshine. The sea was a good-humored presence, a playmate, and not at all mysterious.

In between, they talked, she and Gran. Gran took her through the house and showed her everything, opening drawers and chests and wardrobes. For the house was full of treasures: a fluffy boll of cotton from Antigua; a brittle red lobster's claw from Maine; a huge, rough, curling shell from Puerto Rico that had a flaring ear lined with shiny pink as delicate as china; a little pig from Haiti, carved from satinwood; a length of gaudy cloth from Trinidad; a snuff box from New York City with a picture on it of Martin Van Buren, an old campaign souvenir. And with each treasure came stories from Gran that filled Jenny's head with rich, exotic pictures of the color and slow heat of the Caribbean, the noise and bustle of the northern American ports.

In one of the trunks there was a miniature tin trumpet and a wooden cannon, toys that had been her father's when he was young. She lingered over them, delighted to find that the trumpet still gave out a reedy bleat when she blew it. But Gran had no stories to go with these treasures. She only said, "George was such an active child. How he loved the sea when he was little!"

"He doesn't love it now," said Jenny. "Why not, Gran?"

Gran's face took on a shadow. "He was there with me the day the *Amaryllis* sank. He adored his father, and I suppose he just never got over it. He went away to Springfield soon after, and didn't even try to understand." She put the trumpet and the cannon back into the trunk and took out an object wrapped in paper. "Here. Look at this. Isn't this remarkable?"

The object, unwrapped, turned out to be a plaster sea gull, its wings arched, ready for flight. But as

Jenny turned it round in her hands, it looked like a wave, too, with dipping curls of foam. "Is it meant to be a bird," she asked, "or . . ."

"Good for you!" said Gran. "It's both. It's lots of things. Nicholas Irving made it. It was a model for a bigger piece, a statue he tried to carve once from marble. Poor Nicholas! Bring it downstairs if you like. I haven't looked at it for years. Anyway, it's time for lunch."

This had been Friday morning. The first week was coming to an end, and Jenny, stuffed with wind and sea, was sunburned and deeply contented. The days had been richer than any she had ever known, and except for occasional reminders of some old quarrel between Gran and her father, she was completely happy. But after lunch on this Friday, the sky turned heavy. It began to drizzle, and as so often happens when the weather changes, the mood changed, too, helped along by a visitor who soured the calm of Gran's house like a drop of vinegar in cream.

Jenny answered the knock at the door, and was surprised to find, instead of the egg man or the green-grocer, a woman dressed in the very height of fashion:

a tailored suit of dark, ribbed silk, its skirt draped in rich folds over her hips, and ending in an underskirt of pleated yellow that just brushed the tops of smart black-leather boots. "And who have we here, I wonder?" said the woman, as if all outdoors belonged to her and Jenny had just knocked at *her* door to be let out into it.

"I'm Geneva Reade," said Jenny, suddenly aware of her own bare feet and untidy gingham pinafore. "Did you want to see my grandmother?"

"Grandmother!" exclaimed the woman. She laughed, tilting her head so that the yellow plume on her black felt hat bobbed and waved. Her face, though it was no longer young, was extremely pretty: a round face, dimpled, framed in becoming waves of gray-brown hair drawn back over small, neat ears. "A grandmother? But, of course. It *has* been that long."

"Who's there?" called Gran from the kitchen.

"Hello, Geneva," the woman called back, as she came in, furling her black umbrella. "You'll never guess! Come here at once and see!"

Gran came stumping into the parlor and stopped dead. "Isabel! Heaven help me, it's Isabel Cooper, isn't it?"

"Right and wrong," said the woman gaily. "Isabel

Owen for a good long time now. What *have* you done to yourself, Geneva? Sprained your ankle?"

"Broke it," said Gran. "What in the world are you doing here?"

"We're on our way down to Greenville, my dear. But Harley had some tiresome business or other to do in town, so I said, 'Harley, I'll just go and see some of my old friends,' so he dropped me here. He'll only be a short time, but I did so want to see you, Geneva, before we went our way. Why, it's been ages and ages!"

"Sit down, Isabel," said Gran without enthusiasm, lowering herself into her own chair. "This is my namesake, George's daughter. Geneva, this is Mrs.— uh—Owen, did you say? I used to know her long ago, when she lived here in town."

"How do you do," said Jenny, bobbing a small curtsy in her best Springfield manner.

"George's child!" said the woman. "I declare! I can't imagine little George all grown up. Geneva, she's the image of you, the very image."

"Yes, she is," said Gran complacently. "She's here to help me while my ankle mends."

"I see," said Mrs. Owen, and instantly lost interest in Jenny, who sat down across the room to watch this fascinating visitor. "Geneva, you've hardly changed at all. I'd have known you anywhere. Why, it's amazing how well you've kept over the years."

"One foot in the grave," said Gran. "You've kept well yourself, I see."

"Yes, but, my dear, I *am* a ways behind you, after all. Twenty-five years younger, at least, if my memory serves."

"Twenty," said Gran, "but never mind. We're both past our prime."

The woman frowned briefly, and then turned sunny again. "Oh, well," she said carelessly, "whatever *that* may mean. I'm sure I don't think of myself as one whit different from what I used to be. Happy times, Geneva, the old days here!"

"Yes, you were quite a belle," said Gran dryly.

The woman dimpled. "I was, rather, wasn't I! But, Geneva, here you are still, while I've been out and doing. How ever have you kept yourself amused in this boring old place? I'm sure I couldn't wait to get away!"

"Why should I leave?" said Gran. "This is my home."

"Of course," said Mrs. Owen, turning solemn on the instant. "The Captain. Forgive me. You know, I was just sure you'd never marry again. Here you sit, and unless I'm mistaken, you haven't changed a thing in this room since the Captain . . . that is—"

"No," said Gran. "Nothing's been changed. Why should I change it? I like it this way."

The woman rose from her chair and wandered about the room, picking things up, looking at them, putting them down again. "I remember that teapot," she said, pointing to the china on the mantelpiece. "You let my mother borrow it once, and I came down to get it for her. Remember? It was the day of my sixteenth birthday party, and the hired girl had broken *our* teapot that very morning. Dear me! It seems like yesterday."

"Close to forty years ago," said Gran, "if it's a day."

"I'm sure I don't know why you keep harping on exact numbers of years, Geneva," said Mrs. Owen. "It's such a tiresome habit. Dear me, what's this?" She paused at a side table where, before lunch, Jenny had set down the plaster sea gull that looked like a wave. "Geneva, what in the world is this old thing?"

"Do you mean to tell me, Isabel," said Gran, her ironic enjoyment of this visitor drying up on the instant, "that you don't remember? Of course you do.

I can't imagine why you bother to pretend you don't. That's Nicholas Irving's work, as you very well know —the model he made for the statue."

"Nicholas Irving? Oh. Dear me. Of course. Now I remember. What a funny duck he was. Yes, I do remember something about a statue."

"I should think you would," said Gran. "Don't try to play your little games with me, missy. You remember it perfectly well, and now that I come to think of it, I dare say that's why you came here today—to see if you'd been forgiven at last. A guilty conscience can be very troublesome, I've heard."

"Well, you're entirely wrong about that, Geneva," said the woman resentfully. "I don't in the least feel guilty. But I might have guessed you'd still be blaming me for what happened to Nicholas."

"He loved you, heaven help him," said Gran, "and you let him think you loved him back. He was making that statue for *you*, and then you laughed at it, Isabel. You laughed, and broke his heart."

"Well, I'm sure it wasn't *my* fault if he cared for me," said Mrs. Owen, her round face puckering a little. "*I* couldn't help it. Lots of boys cared for me, and *they* didn't go and drown themselves."

"Nicholas wasn't 'lots of boys,'" said Gran. "Nicholas was special."

"I'm sure you see it that way, Geneva," said the woman, "but I couldn't go and marry *everyone*, now, could I? Anyway, Nicholas was so . . . solemn. Oh, I liked him at first, but after a while he just got too . . . well, too solemn, as I say. About as much fun as an old sheep. And I never could see what that silly statue had to do with anything."

Gran started to speak, stopped, and turned to look at Jenny, who was sitting open-mouthed, listening. "Geneva," she said, "I'd very much appreciate it if you'd go up to your room for a while. I'll call you down later."

"But, Gran!" Jenny protested, and then, seeing the look in her grandmother's eye, she said, almost meekly, "All right." She went out into the hall and up the stairs, as slowly as she dared, but there was silence in the parlor, and once in her room, when the conversation started up again, she could hear nothing more than a murmur from the two women. After a time, however, their voices rose suddenly and the words were audible.

"Listen to the pot calling the kettle black!" cried

the visitor. "You're a fine one, Geneva Reade, to talk about sparing a person's feelings! Everyone knows how you neglected that boy of yours after the Captain drowned. Why, you never cared a straw for George. It was just the Captain, the Captain, always the Captain, until—"

"Leave this house, Isabel Cooper," Gran thundered, "and never come back. I don't ever want to see you again."

Crisp footsteps in the hall, and then: "But, Geneva, it's raining outside, and Harley isn't back yet. You can't expect me to—"

"Yes, I can," said Gran, and Jenny could imagine the grim expression on her grandmother's face. "Goodbye, Isabel."

The sound of the door opening and closing. A moment of silence. Next the thump as Gran's crutch swung her back to the parlor. Then nothing but the rain and the slosh of waves. But Jenny sat on her father's bed, and the visitor's words hung in her ears, so that she did not hear anything else. "You never cared a straw for George." Could it be true? And all at once the little tin trumpet seemed the saddest thing in the world to her. What chance had its thin sound ever had, trying to be heard above the tide?

When Jenny came downstairs again, she found Gran standing at the window behind her chair, staring out at the sea. Searching for something to say, Jenny managed at last, "She's not very nice, that woman who was here."

"No," said Gran, without turning around. "She isn't, and wasn't. The face of an angel, even now, but in no way like an angel otherwise."

"Did Nicholas Irving really drown himself because of her?" asked Jenny.

"So they say," said Gran. She came away from the window and sat down in her chair. She looked exhausted. "Geneva, people do strange things for love sometimes. You're old enough to realize that."

A silence fell between them. Jenny fingered a fold

of her pinafore, and then she said, with difficulty, "Gran, didn't you love my father?"

"You mustn't think such things," said Gran stiffly. "Forget you ever heard it. That woman—Isabel—she's a fool. She understands nothing at all. The only thing she cares about is what others think of her. To people like that, the rest of the world is there just to hold up a mirror for them to see their own reflection in. She never understood poor Nicholas, and she doesn't understand anything about your father and me. He's my son. Of course I love him. We don't agree on certain things, that's all. Put it out of your mind." She turned away and took up the almanac. "High tide at five o'clock. An hour from now," she announced, staring down at the page. Then she closed the almanac and laid it aside. "This rain is going to be with us for a while, Geneva," she said. "You'll need something to keep you dry. Go upstairs to the back bedroom and look in the bottom of that big trunk, the one where we found the sea gull. I think there's an old oilskin there somewhere that your father had when he was about your age. And a sou'wester, too."

Upstairs, Jenny knelt before the trunk and lifted its great domed lid. The trumpet and the cannon were lying on top of the accumulation inside, but she did not pick them up again. Instead, she thrust a hand down under the layers of odds and ends, searching for the slick feel of the oilskin. At last she found it and, as carefully as she could, began to pull it up and out, trying not to disturb the things resting on top of it. But this appeared to be impossible, and as she gave the oilskin a final yank to free it, it brought up with it, caught in the stiffness of a too-long-folded sleeve, a small, square leather box which tumbled out onto the floor.

She left the oilskin dangling from the trunk and, picking up the box, tried to open it. There was a little metal knob sticking out of its front side and this she pressed firmly. At first nothing happened, but a stronger jab released an inner catch, and the lid sprang open. The box was lined with purple velvet, and there, resting in a depression that fit it exactly, lay a wafer-thin gold pocket watch. It was a handsome thing, much more handsome than the watches for sale in her father's store, the kind he carried himself: of some metal that was silver-colored but not silver, and thick as a thumb. Jenny eased the gold watch out of its nest and turned it over. The back was engraved with curling vines and leaves, and in the center a small square, left plain, was marked with the single initial R.

Jenny had often opened the back of her father's watch to look at the works, so intricate, fitted so precisely into their round, neat skull. She pried this one open now with a fingernail, and peered in. And then her eye fell on the inside of the lifted back, and she saw that it, too, was engraved:

MORGAN READE 1818

GEORGE MORGAN READE 1857

George Morgan Reade. That was her father! She stood up, tucking the stiff, creased oilskin under her arm, and went downstairs, the watch cupped carefully in one palm. "Gran," she said, going into the parlor, "look what I found! It's got my father's name in it."

Gran had been studying the almanac again, and looked up from it vaguely, as if it were an effort to bring herself out of her thoughts. But when Jenny put the watch into her hand, her eyes cleared. "Dear heaven!" she exclaimed. "It's your grandfather's watch."

"But it has Papa's name in it, too," said Jenny. "Look—it's on the inside of the lid."

Gran opened the back and stared at the names engraved there. "Yes. I remember now. Your grandfather got this watch on his twenty-first birthday, from *his* father. But he never carried it with him when he went to sea. He used to say it was too special, that it might get lost or stolen, and that he wanted to save it for . . . George. For George's twenty-first birthday. He had the name and date put in long before, to be ready."

"But, Gran! Papa's way past twenty-one by now. Why didn't you ever give it to him?"

"I forgot," said Gran. "I clean forgot all about it. When the time came, your father had been a long time in Springfield. I remember sending him a letter, to wish him a happy birthday, but I just plain forgot about this."

"It would've meant a lot to Papa, I expect, to have it," said Jenny disapprovingly. "You should've remembered."

"Now you're angry," said Gran, and the tired look came back to her face.

"Well, I just don't understand it," said Jenny. "What's the trouble with you and Papa, anyway?"

"Geneva, dear child," said Gran, "I don't know how to explain it to you, or even if I should try. But —well—your father, he's a fine man, but he just doesn't see. After the *Amaryllis* went down, he kept saying to me, 'It's over.' And he wanted me to move back to Springfield and start a new life. But I didn't want a new life. I wanted this one, and I didn't believe it was over. I wanted to stay here where I could be close to . . . the ship, where I could wait. Your grandfather and I—what we felt for each other doesn't just stop. Remember what we talked about the first night you were here? There's another world around us, Geneva, around us all the time, and here I can be closer to it. But your father—he doesn't sense the other world around him; he doesn't see that things don't end. If he did, he wouldn't be so frightened. Ever since his father drowned, he's been terrified of endings. He thinks of the sea the way other people think of graveyards, and he can't stand this place because it keeps reminding him. That's why he ran away —to run away from endings. He was very young, and some people thought I was wrong to allow the separation. But what could I have done? He couldn't stay here, and I couldn't leave."

She paused and ran a fingertip over the names engraved inside the lid of the gold watch. And then she said, "This watch, now—it's like a sign in itself, isn't it? A sign from father to son. The numbers stand on the face in an endless circle, and the hands will keep going round and round when we wind it up. But George wouldn't have seen it like that. He'd only have seen an old watch that had stopped—time come to an end—and he wouldn't have wanted to have it. Do you understand?"

Jenny stood staring at Gran, and could feel herself pulled between them, her father and her grandmother. "I don't know," she said.

Gran stared back at her and then she pulled herself up out of her chair and stood tall. "Enough," she said. "Come. High tide."

And so, another useless search, another supper. But things felt very different. The rain continued, filling in the chinks of silence that *would* fall between them, Gran and Jenny, no matter how hard they tried to keep a conversation going. Bedtime came as a welcome relief, and Jenny, protected by an earnest wish not to think about the watch, and the little tin trumpet, and the ugly words of the pretty Mrs. Owen, went to sleep almost at once.

When Gran next called her, Jenny woke to find that the windows of her room were touched faintly with light, the pale beginnings of dawn. There was scarcely a breath of wind. She went to the window and saw that the sea had been transformed. It was hung with a thin fog, against which the rain still fell, straight down, with a whispering sound, hushed and dim. Downstairs, Gran was waiting with the oilskin and Jenny put it on obediently, but they both moved quietly, as if there were someone or something near that must not be awakened or disturbed. "We won't need the lantern," said Gran in a low voice. "It's almost light. Geneva, I have a feeling that perhaps, this time . . . Come, let's go out and begin."

The beach was ghostly, muffled, in the silvery halflight. The warm rain was so fine that it was almost a mist, but it raised tiny knobs on the surface of the swelling water, water that rolled so gently it did not crest, but merely flattened, sighing, on the sand, sliding far up to the bottom of the bluff with only the barest film of bubbles. The far horizon had vanished in the fog, and the swells seemed to be coming in from nowhere, only to this place and nowhere else, glinting with that same pale silver light that was part dawn, part fog, part rain. Jenny started off along the dark strip of sand with her hands deep in the pockets of the oilskin, feeling as if she were still asleep and dreaming, carrying the dream along around her.

For the fog gave way ahead and closed behind her as she went, and the now-familiar landmarks, as they swam into focus, looked strange: the boulder, gleaming now with rain; the withered scrub-pine stump decked with moisture-beaded spiderwebs; the rotted dock, its far end faint in fog out over the water; and finally another bluff that marked the limit of that arm of the search, soft now, its rough grass leaning and heavy with raindrops. She paused here, blinking, her cheeks wet under the brim of the old sou'wester. She could feel the silence and the waiting everywhere. And then she turned and started back.

She had reached the scrub-pine stump again when she saw it: a dark something floating just within her sight, where the sea faded into the fog. It rose and fell on the soundless, shifting water, and with each swell it was brought a little closer to shore, a little closer to where she stood. "Driftwood," she suggested to herself, but it did not look like driftwood. Its shape seemed too regular, too smooth. As she stood there, her eyes wide, straining to see more clearly, the wind lifted and the rain began to fall a little harder, digging tiny pockmarks in the sand. Riding a taller swell, the object rolled, submerged, bobbed up again, and Jenny saw a touch of color on its surface. "It isn't driftwood," she said aloud. "It's—something else."

The object, floating now in sight, now lost between the swells, came nearer and nearer. Suddenly Jenny could wait no longer. She waded out, deeper and deeper, until at last she stood in water to her waist. Heaves of sea lifted the oilskin up around her and dragged at her, but her eyes were fixed on the object, and at last it washed into her reaching arms. Clutching it, she struggled back to shore, and stood there in the rain, holding the thing, staring down at it.

It was made of wood and it was heavy with years of seeping water, but she saw at once what it was, in spite of its softened planes and curves, its barely visible residue of paint. She was holding in her arms the carved head of a woman, split at an angle across the lower face so that only a portion of the mouth remained. But the eyes, under heavy brows, were lidded and calm, the nose long and narrow, the section of mouth curved upward in a smile. And the hair, swept down from the brow in deep-carved strands, still held bright fragments of dark red color.

Staring at the head, Jenny swallowed hard. And then she began to run down the beach, clumsy in the flapping oilskin, her heels thudding over the firm, wet sand, holding the wooden head tight against her chest. "Gran!" she cried. "Gran! I've got something!" The fog opened out ahead of her, and at last she could see her grandmother standing on the little bluff, a dim shape under a big umbrella. "Gran!" she cried again.

"Quick!" came Gran's voice. "Quick! Oh, Lord, it's come! Yes, *yes*, child, bring it to me!"

Jenny arrived breathless at the bottom of the bluff and struggled up, and Gran, dropping her crutch, flinging aside the umbrella, reached out and seized the wooden head. She took one look at it and sank down on the old bench, clasping the head to her bosom, rocking back and forth. "Geneva," she cried, "do you know what this is? Do you see? It's my head, from the ship! Heaven be praised, he's sent me a sign at last!" Her voice broke and she began to weep, her words coming slow between deep, gasping breaths. "It's the figurehead, Geneva—from my darling—

from the *Amaryllis*—sent up from the bottom of the sea."

And the wind, rising, whispered around them: *True to yo-o-o-ou.*

The rest of that day, and the next and the next, were as confused and cloudy as the first days had been calm and bright. Outside, the sky hung low, clouds drifting over clouds, and the rain fell softly, continuously, turning the sea and beach into a blur. Inside, Gran was feverish. She would talk, excitedly, and then lapse into silence, drop off to sleep for a moment, and wake to talk again. Jenny did not know what to do with her, and a vague alarm moved in to tremble in her stomach. The head from the *Amaryllis* lay on the table beside Gran's chair in the parlor, and the calm smile on its carved face was more like the Gran Jenny knew than this agitated woman who sat, stood, stumped about, sat again, dozed exhausted, doing none of these for more than five minutes at a time, it seemed.

Jenny took over the cooking, producing from Gran's unfamiliar stores peculiar meals whose inharmonious parts were never ready at the same moment, never ready to the same degree of doneness; and she carried them in to the parlor on a tray, but Gran would scarcely touch them. "Geneva," she would say, "did I ever tell you the story of how—" and would begin a tale told once so far that hour and twice the hour before, of her life in the old days with the Captain. For she called him "the Captain" now, not "your grandfather," and she talked of nothing, no one, else, putting out her hand again and again to touch the wooden head. And then, in the middle of the story, her voice would fade and she would fall asleep, her head bowed down on her chest.

It was clear from the brightness of her eyes and the flush on her cheeks that she was ill. But Jenny did not know how to find the doctor and was in any case afraid to leave her grandmother alone while she went out to look, for she feared that now, in addition to the fever, Gran might really be going mad. The building in Springfield, the one with the dark, barred windows, was never far from her thoughts. "If the doctor comes," she worried, "he'll see how it is with her.

He'll send for my father and they'll take her away."
And so she waited, helplessly.

But at the end of the third day, late in the afternoon, she tiptoed in to the parlor from the kitchen and found that Gran was truly asleep at last, her breathing deep and regular. The flush was gone from her face, and her hands lay relaxed in her lap. The fever, at least, had passed. Weak with relief, Jenny smoothed the quilt over her grandmother's knees, tucking it under, and sank down on a footstool near the window. Outside, the rain still fell, the swells still spilled across the sodden beach, and Jenny realized that she had not left the house since the day of the discovery. There had been no watching for the tides, no searching up and back along the sand. There was, of course, no need for searching now.

Then, for the first time, she turned and looked—really looked—at the wooden head lying on the table next to her. Reaching out a hand, she ran her finger-tips over its water-softened cheek. The surface, dry-ing a little in the warmth of the lamp beside it, felt fuzzy, and the fragments of red paint in the deep-carved strands of hair were curling here and there, turning up their edges as they, too, dried in the lamplight. The head was real. There could be no doubt about that. The place where it had split from the rest of the body was lighter in color, and rougher, as if the break were recent: the wood was raw, not mellowed yet by the constant caress of salt water.

Yes, the head was real. It had been a part of the *Amaryllis*, and now it was here. It had come—here. A queer coincidence. Perhaps. But it was here. Gran stirred in her sleep and her mouth curved into a smile, and Jenny saw how much her grandmother's face still looked like this younger, wooden face carved so long ago—strong, handsome, a very good face. And all at once she remembered something the terrible and pretty Mrs. Owen had said to Gran: "She's the image of you, Geneva—the very image."

The very image? Did she, too, then, have a very good face? After all? Not ugly? Would someone, some shadowy someone, love her someday the way her grandfather had loved Gran? Or perhaps still loved Gran from . . . wherever he was? Unexpectedly, she found that she was blushing. "That's silly," she said aloud, and stood up, moved about the room, plumping pillows, bustling, embarrassed. But her heart had a new lightness, and the trembling in her stomach had disappeared.

Gran woke in the morning, after the third long night in her chair, pale but refreshed. "What are we doing down here in the parlor?" she demanded as Jenny, sitting up from her own sleep on the sofa, greeted her. "Good grief, I'm stiff as a board."

"You've been sick, Gran," said Jenny. "I was so worried—how do you feel?"

"Well, now, let's see," said Gran doubtfully, patting herself here and there. "I seem to be all right, but I'm hungry as a bear. Yes, I remember now. Foolish old woman, to stand so long outside in the rain. And yet" —she turned to gaze at the wooden head—"it wasn't entirely foolish."

They were quiet then. Jenny came to stand by Gran, and they both looked at the head, which smiled back serenely. "I knew it would happen," said Gran, "and it did." She put a gentle hand on her grand-daughter's arm. "Geneva," she said, "remember this: nothing is impossible."

There followed three lighthearted days, in spite of the steady rain cocooning them, lighthearted for Jenny because Gran was all right again, better, in fact, than she had been before; lighthearted for Gran because her dearest wish had been granted. All of her old intensity, her obsession with the tides, was gone, to uncover, by its absence, a great capacity for pleasure.

She taught Jenny how to play German whist; they read aloud; they made salt-water taffy. A new trunk was opened, revealing hats and dresses in the opulent style of the 1830's and 40's, and for hours they played at dressing up. Gran pulled out one tall-brimmed bonnet with plumes and ribbons and ruffled white lace, and, clapping it on her head, went to see herself in a mirror. "Well, it looked all right in its heyday," she said, laughing at her reflection. "Or in *my* heyday, I should say. Wait. I know. Come with me." She stumped to the parlor and, picking up the wooden head, placed the bonnet over the carved hair lovingly. "That's the way it looked, more or less." The head smiled indulgently. "No," said Gran, removing the bonnet and laying the head back, gently, in its place. "What's the matter with me? Blasphemy, almost. But your grandfather gave me this bonnet. How he would laugh to see the figurehead wearing it! He was a great laugher, that man. Everything amused him."

Jenny remembered, then, her father's sober face.

"Gran," she said slowly, "if Papa could see the head, would it make him feel better? Would it make him love the sea again, and not be so afraid?"

Gran turned and looked at her. "When he comes for you, the end of next week," she said thoughtfully, "we'll show it to him. And give him the watch. And see."

And so it came to a Friday again, and still the rain fell. The beach had a drowned, abandoned look, and in the afternoon Jenny, growing restless, put on the old oilskin and ventured out to look around. She had entirely lost track of the tides, but the sea seemed to her to have sunk beyond even its farthest point, slapping sullenly at the hard, ridged sand. Below the line of soggy seaweed, she found a sharp trail of new clawprints, like little forks, etched cleanly in the sand, and following them she spotted at last the sea gull responsible, waddling discontentedly some distance ahead. His feathers looked bedraggled and askew, like an old shirt, ragged and none too clean. But when he heard her approaching, he opened perfect wings and, transformed, lifted into the air, beating off above the water, powerful and sure. Somehow his flight from her made her feel alien and wistful. She hung her head and started back along the empty beach, higher up, above the tide line. It seemed, now, to be a kind of trespassing to mark the smoother sand, where the gull had walked, with feet that did not belong there.

It was because of this higher route home that she noticed the deep prints of a man's heavy boots, stretching ahead of her near the edge of the sand where the wet grass leaned. The rims of the prints were softened from the rain, no longer crisp, as the gull's prints had been, so Jenny knew that the man who had made them had come along some time before. But still she felt queer to see them there. Abruptly, she lost the sense that she was the intruder here. Instead, it now began to feel as if she herself—and Gran—had been intruded upon, on this sand that was theirs alone. She hurried back to the house and said to Gran, "There's been a man walking on our beach."

And Gran, putting down her mending, frowned and said, "Seward."

At supper Gran said musingly, "I wonder if Seward knows the head has come."

"But how could he?" Jenny asked, surprised. "And, Gran, I don't see why he should care about it, anyway. Unless," she added quickly, "if he's your friend and would be glad to see you happy."

"He's not exactly . . . a friend," said Gran.

"Oh," said Jenny. A vague apprehension filled her and she asked, a little timidly, "Is he a bad person?"

Gran looked hard at her, as if she were trying to see inside her head. "Geneva," she said, "it's not a question of good or bad. It's a question of whether he's . . ." She paused.

"Whether he's what?" asked Jenny, frowning, fearful of what the answer would be.

"Finish your supper," said Gran. "We'll talk in the parlor afterwards. I can see I'd better tell you the whole story."

The parlor, with the lamps turned up and a fresh fire popping in the grate, should have been cozy and secure, but Jenny sat nervously on the sofa, opposite Gran's chair, and folded her hands. "I feel the way I do at home when we tell ghost stories," she said as her grandmother eased herself down and laid the crutch on the floor.

"Well," said Gran, lifting her eyebrows, "in a way that's what we're going to do."

"I don't believe in ghosts, though," said Jenny. "Do you?"

"I don't know," said Gran. "I didn't when I was your age, but now . . . Geneva, you see that the sign has come, don't you?"

"Yes," said Jenny, "but . . ."

"I know," said Gran. "You believe it's accidental. Well, perhaps you're right, perhaps not. Nevertheless, the head from the *Amaryllis* has come home after thirty years, and it lies here on this table, in plain sight. And there's something more about it you didn't

notice, being unfamiliar with such things. It's got no
barnacles on it, and no signs of rotting. Keep that in
mind, Geneva, while I talk."

She settled her ankle more comfortably on the
hassock and leaned back. "Do you remember that I
told you about Nicholas Irving, and how he drowned
himself not long after the *Amaryllis* sank?"

"Yes," said Jenny. "Because of that woman who
was here."

"Isabel Cooper," said Gran. "Yes. Because at first
she pretended to be fond of him, but then, later, she
laughed at him to his face, laughed at his work and at
his love for her. We thought at first, when he disappeared, that he'd gone away—inland, perhaps, or
down the coast. It wasn't until two days later that his
dinghy was found, washed up. Without him in it.
Still, some people thought it had drifted loose by itself
and that Nicholas was holed up somewhere, licking
his wounds. But he didn't come back, and at last some
of his friends went to his workshop to see if he'd left
any messages or clues. They found all his tools lying
about, and another figurehead for some other ship,
only half finished. His clothes were there, food stores,
everything. And the marble statue he'd been working
on, it was still there, too, but it looked as if he'd tried

to smash it. It was all chipped and scarred with chisel marks." She sighed. "He was . . . temperamental. Another man might have squared his shoulders and gone ahead with his life in spite of being unlucky in love, but not Nicholas. He was completely addled over Isabel."

"Well," said Jenny, "I guess she was very pretty."

"Yes, she was," Gran returned, "but Nicholas should have known that wasn't much all by itself. 'Pretty' doesn't mean 'good,' you know, Geneva. Real life isn't like fairy tales. 'Pretty' simply means that by accident you've got things arranged on your outside in an extra-pleasing manner. It doesn't tell a thing about your inside. Still, Nicholas was temperamental, as I said, notional, the way they say all artists are, and beauty was important to him. But we were very fond of him. He came here often. He was almost ten years older than your father, but he was rather like a son to us, and sometimes when your grandfather was off on a voyage, he'd come and read to George and me, or take a hand of whist. He was a good boy, and very, very gifted." She sighed again, remembering, and shook her head. "His friends found a note in his workshop. It said, 'I can't go on. Look for me in the sea.' "

"That's sad!" said Jenny, much moved by this romantic tale.

"It's absurd," Gran contradicted severely. "A terrible, terrible waste, and all for nothing."

"Still," said Jenny dreamily, liking the story anyway, "I feel sorry for him."

"It's not a happy story, certainly," said Gran, the hardness of her tone melting away. "A month or two after his disappearance—his drowning—whatever—one night when I was walking on the beach—remember, I was newly widowed then, and half crazy with it, heaven help me—I was walking on the beach, it was one of those nights when the moon is very bright, and I was wandering along, worried about George, who'd gone away to Springfield to live with your Great-aunt Jane, and I was longing for something from the *Amaryllis*, thinking about the sinking, trying to figure it out, when all at once I noticed a man coming toward me. He looked familiar, somehow, his clothes and his way of walking, and I cried out, 'Nicholas!' And it *was* Nicholas, but he was different."

"Different how?" asked Jenny, fearful again of the reply.

"It was his eyes, mostly. They didn't have that fiery

light in them any more," said Gran. "They were quiet. And he had a beard, too. He tried to ignore me, to go on past me, but I spoke to him again, and he stopped and said, as if he were a stranger, 'Not Nicholas, ma'am. My name is Seward.' "

"Seward!" Jenny exclaimed.

"Yes," said Gran. "And for a moment I thought I'd made a mistake. But he raised his hand up to his beard and I saw the scar on his thumb where his chisel had slipped once long before when he was working. No, it was Nicholas, all right, and I said so. So we walked together and he told me . . ."

"What?" Jenny urged.

"Geneva, you may believe it or not, just as you choose. *I* believed it, and I'll tell you why in a minute. He told me he'd rowed the dinghy out, far out to sea, the night of the day that Isabel laughed at him. And he stowed the oars, stood up, and flung himself overboard. He was so determined to drown that when he sank he opened his mouth and tried to breathe the water into his lungs, but in the next moment he came to the surface again and began to choke. In that moment he forgot about Isabel and wanted to stay alive after all, so he looked around for the dinghy, but it was gone."

"Gone?" said Jenny, breathless. "You mean, disappeared?"

"So he told me," said Gran. "He began trying to swim, but found that he couldn't, somehow, and instead he sank again and kept on sinking, in spite of kicking and trying to come back up. He described the water to me as voices, talking to him, pulling him down and down. And all he could think of was how much he didn't want to drown. He tried to speak to the voices, and found that he could, and he argued with them all the way to the bottom. Yes. He went all the way to the bottom. And he told me, Geneva, that when he got to the bottom, he saw the *Amaryllis*."

"Oh, Gran!" said Jenny, forgetting for the moment that she was supposed to be making up her mind about all this.

"Yes," said Gran. "It was the *Amaryllis*, and it was moving over the sea bottom. Its lamps were lit and there were men working on the deck, though he told me he was too far away to see who they were."

"But how did he know it was the *Amaryllis*, if he was so far away?" asked Jenny.

"Why," said Gran, "he recognized the figurehead. There was light, he told me, coming from the face, from the eyes, and he recognized it, even through the blur of water. And all the time the voices kept talking to him and he kept arguing, saying he didn't want to stay down there, and at last it seemed as if a bargain had been struck, and the next thing he knew, he was lying on the beach in the dark, and he was completely dry. As if he'd never been in the water at all. And he told me that he knew he wasn't Nicholas Irving any more, but someone—something—else; that he would be called Seward now because it meant 'guardian of the sea.' And he realized that he'd promised, in exchange for being returned, to walk along the beaches and give back to the sea anything that it valued—that was the word, 'valued'—that had somehow been washed ashore. And that if he didn't keep his promise, he'd be brought back down to the bottom of the sea again and kept there."

"Drowned after all," said Jenny.

"Yes," said Gran. "Drowned after all. And then he told me that he knew, as clearly as if he'd been told— in fact, he believed he had been told—that your grandfather wanted more than anything else to send a sign to me—that his desire was very strong—and that he, Seward, would have to watch and make sure that, if a sign was sent, it was something I'd be allowed to keep."

Jenny frowned, trying to picture the scene under-water. "He really saw the ship on the bottom," she said.

"Yes," said Gran. "Sailing. Keeping watch. The sea bottom was covered with treasure, he told me, and there were lots of wrecked ships, too, great ruined hulls, lying down there forsaken, full of holes and rotting away. But the *Amaryllis*, and all the ships with figureheads, are kept whole and clean, he said, to sail on the bottom and guard the treasure."

All at once Jenny could not accept the story. Springfield asserted itself, and she said, "I don't be-lieve it."

"You don't?"

"No. It's crazy. That man—Seward, or whoever he is—he must have dreamed it."

"Very well," said Gran calmly. "There's one last piece to the story. As we stood there on the sand in the moonlight, talking, two of your grandfather's friends came down from the grass above us. One of them took my arm and said, 'Geneva, come back with us. We've been looking for you. You know the Cap-tain wouldn't want you to wander out here night after night all by yourself.' And I turned around to them and I said, 'But I'm not by myself,' and they said, in this pitying sort of way, 'Come with us now. You must try to get hold of yourself.' I turned back, and Seward had walked away, on down the beach. 'No,' I said, 'I want to stay here and talk to Nicholas,' and I called to him to come back. And one of the men said, 'Geneva, please, there's no one there.' "

"You mean they didn't see him?" said Jenny.

"No," said Gran, "they didn't see him. But I couldn't see him, either, very well, by that time, he'd gone so far. So I thought, well, perhaps they just hadn't noticed him, so I pointed to the row of footprints he'd made as he walked away. They were very clear in the moonlight. And I said, 'Look. See the footprints? I haven't been alone. It was Nicholas, and we've been walking.' And then one of the men put his arm around me and said, 'Geneva, you're exhausted and you're making yourself sick. There aren't any footprints there.' "

"But, Gran!" Jenny began, eyes wide.

"Wait," Gran interrupted. "Seward—or Nicholas —has been walking this beach for thirty years, and no one's ever seen him but me. Him *or* his footprints. Not then, on that night, or at any time thereafter."

They sat staring at each other in silence. At last Jenny said, "But, Gran, *I* saw him—and I saw his footprints, too."

"Yes, child," said Gran. "You did."

Later Jenny lay in bed, eyes wide and staring into the dark. She kept thinking about Seward, but she did not want to think about him. If the rain would only stop, if the sun would shine tomorrow, everything would seem a great deal more reasonable. This place, this house—she saw more clearly than ever, now, that it stood at the edge of another world, at the edge where the things she understood and the things beyond her understanding began to merge and blur. That other world—it brought on transformations, and its blurring edge was marked by the hemline of the sea.

Still, even the sea seemed simple in the sunshine. Funny how clear, bright daylight made you laugh at phantoms. They vanished, fled away like smoke, under the sun's round, candid eye. Yes, that was the thing: sunshine to light the corners.

But there was no sunshine next morning. The rain had stopped at last, but the sky was still hung with gray, against which new humps of vapor hurried by, changing their shapes and rolling as they went. After breakfast, Gran turned the pages of the almanac and read, aloud:

> *Final days of August*
> *Usher in September.*
> *Autumn equinox ahead—*
> *Stormy seas. Remember.*

"Stormy seas!" said Jenny, discouraged. "Does that mean it's going to rain again?"

"It's coming into that time of year, Geneva," said Gran. "Always bad weather at the equinox. Is it getting on your nerves?"

"A little," said Jenny.

"I know," said Gran. "Moss in the bones. Still, I like it, somehow."

"Better than when the sun is out?"

"Yes, I really do. It's much more interesting, I've always thought. Come, let's bake a cake. That should cheer you up."

Jenny cracked the eggs—twelve of them, a whole dozen days of labor for some unknown, dedicated hen—and beat their slippery whites into a rigid cloud of foam. She had beaten egg whites often before, but now she saw the process as yet another transformation. She sifted the flour, measured the sugar, watched as Gran folded everything into a batter smooth and pale as thickened cream. Transformations again. And the humble dailiness of these activities only increased the knowledge that, at some undetermined point, her world had slid away a final barrier and allowed that other world to merge with it at last, like the fog moving in from nowhere, into the air she breathed, changing its flavor, giving it a richness it had not had before. Like the scent of the angel-food cake drifting out from the oven to fill the house with promises. Like the head on the parlor table.

While the cake was baking, she found herself wandering again and again to the dining room to look at the drawing of the *Amaryllis*, with its wind-belled sails and thrusting prow, the figurehead tilting un-afraid over a frill of splitting waves, chin lifted to the wide and blank horizon. She tried to picture the ship sailing like this on the sea bottom, and found that she *could* picture it—could easily imagine the heavy silence of the deep, deep water, the schools of little fish flitting soundlessly before the prow, the dim green wavering light surrounding it. And she could see, too, rotting chests and boxes, lids askew, the rocks and sandy bottom glinting here and there with scat-tered treasures. She could picture all this, and more: the shadowy figures on the deck, one of them surely the grandfather she had never seen, striding effort-lessly up and down. Phantoms. But real. And wonder-ful. Why not?

Why not. There was no answer for "why not," ex-cept to say "why not, indeed." And so, at last, accept-ing everything, she said to Gran at lunch, "Will Seward want you to give back the head?"

"I don't know," said Gran. "I've been asking my-self that very question. But if he doesn't know I have it . . . Geneva, perhaps I should put it away somewhere for a while. Just in case." And the deed was done at once, the head nested deep in a drawer of the lowboy in the dining room, the drawer locked, the key dropped into the china teapot on the parlor mantelpiece. "Now," said Gran, "if he should come here—which is very unlikely—he won't discover it. I think we shall be safe. Have another piece of cake. Why, bless my soul, look there! The sun's come out!"

It was true. The house brimmed suddenly with light—hard, yellow light—as if a curtain had been swept aside. From the parlor window after lunch, Jenny saw a sky wiped clean, and polished to a glittering blue. The tide was in, but the sea still seemed sullen, thumping fretfully no more than halfway up the sand as the breeze puffed, dropped, puffed again. She craned her neck to look both ways along the beach, and that was when she saw him—Seward, plodding along, still some distance away, headed in their direction.

Her first thought was: He walks here even when the sun shines! And then: "Gran!" she called. "Come look. He's on the beach again."

Gran came in from the kitchen, where she'd been setting a pot of beans to soak, and stumped up to the window. By this time, Seward had made his way a

great deal closer and his face was lifted. He was looking toward the house.

"Speak of the Devil, and he'll appear," said Gran.

Jenny understood for the first time what this expression really meant, and she shivered a little. "Do
you think he's coming to the house?" she whispered,
as if she feared he'd hear her through the glass.

"He never has before," said Gran. "He'll pass on
by, no doubt."

But he did not pass on by. When he arrived at the
bluff, he turned and, coming up the sand beside it,
paused, pulling at his beard.

"Stand back," Gran murmured. "He'll see us. He's
coming in." She moved away from the window, and
Jenny, turning too, saw that she stood very straight
beside her chair, her chin up. "We'll tell him nothing,
Geneva," she said. "Whatever he asks, we'll tell him
nothing. There. There's his knock. Let him in, child."

If Seward was a ghost, he was a very solid one, a
rather short man, only a few inches taller than Jenny,
but stocky, wearing the same coat she had seen him in
before. His tousled hair and beard were damp and
beaded with sea spray, and the rough-skinned folds
and pouches of his face made him look as if he'd spent
a dozen lifetimes on the beach. He wiped his sandy

boots carefully before he came in, and he stood in the parlor a little awkwardly, keeping his hands in his pockets. He looked about the room, and when his quiet eyes found the plaster sea gull, they flickered briefly and then were quiet once more. "I'm sorry to intrude on you this way, Mrs. Reade," he said, and Jenny thought again how much his low voice sounded like the breeze.

"You're welcome here," said Gran stiffly.

"Something has come," he said.

Gran's fingers tightened on her crutch. "I don't know what you mean," she said.

"It's valued," he said, ignoring her words. He spoke without severity, without any emotion at all. "You must give it back at once."

"I don't know what you mean," Gran repeated. "Nothing has come."

There was a pause, and then his gaze moved to Jenny. "She must give it back, miss," he said.

Jenny found herself unable to speak. She could only stand there clutching the skirt of her pinafore, staring at him.

At last he said, "I'll come again." He turned and stood at the door, waiting. Jenny went and opened it, and he stepped over the sill into the wind, his hair lifting and fluttering. Jenny noticed, then, that much of it was white. "Goodbye, Mrs. Reade," he said without looking back.

"Goodbye, Seward," said Gran with the same stiffness in her voice.

Jenny shut the door behind him and went to the window to watch him move away. Gran said, "He shan't have it." And all the easy calm of the last few days was gone. "I've waited too long. I'll never give it up."

"How did he know?" asked Jenny, feeling again a trembling in her stomach. "What will he do?"

"I don't know," said Gran, "but he shan't have it. If he comes back, Geneva, you're not to let him in."

Early in the evening, after supper, Gran said, "I want to go out and have a look around. Let's go sit on the bench for a while."

"But what if Seward comes back?" Jenny asked her nervously. "What if he's out there now?"

"If he is, he is," said Gran defiantly. "I'm not going to shut myself up in this house because of him. I haven't been out for a week, and I need a breath of air. Get the oilskin, Geneva. The bench will still be damp and we'll need something to sit on."

Outside, settled on the bench, the two sat for a long time without speaking. Gran kept her back straight, standing the crutch upright against her knees, gazing up and down the beach, but there was no one to be seen walking there. Waves came rolling in smoothly, in even rows that smacked the whole length of the beach at once till the sand seemed to ring with them. There was no wind at all.

"Gran," Jenny said at last, "doesn't the sky look funny!" She had been studying it, and had thought at first that it was promising another sunny day tomorrow, but now she was not so sure. From far to the south, high feathers of cloud were fanning up and out from what appeared to be a single point on the horizon, and behind the house they were stained to brilliant orange and scarlet as the sun dropped. "Gran," said Jenny, "look! The clouds are coming in a great big V."

Gran looked up, and her eyes narrowed. After a pause, she said, "Yes. I've seen it like that before. There's a storm somewhere out to sea. Maybe even a hurricane. It's the time of year for it."

"A hurricane!" Jenny exclaimed, and all at once she was dismayed. They heard of such things in Springfield from time to time, and had even felt the fringes of the worst ones in the form of lashing rains and wind. Her father—how pale and quiet he would be until the storm was over! She remembered standing beside him at a window when she was much smaller, watching the raindrops drive against the pane, and he had said, not really to her, "It's a terrible way to go, out at sea in such a storm." And she had thought at the time that by "go" he had meant, simply, "travel," and could not understand the dread she sensed in him. Now she understood it very well, and felt the dread herself. The *Amaryllis* had been lost in a hurricane, and he had stood here, right here where she was sitting now, and watched it all happen. And couldn't do a thing to stop it. "A hurricane!" she repeated. "Will it come here?"

"Perhaps," said Gran, "but I don't think so. They very rarely do. We might get the edges, if there is one, but that's all." Her manner was casual, but there was something behind it that Jenny couldn't read—something hard.

"The air is so quiet," said Jenny uneasily. "There isn't any wind at all."

"Not now," said Gran, "but it may pick up. You mustn't let it frighten you, Geneva. Weather is only weather. It comes and goes."

Jenny was amazed by this response. She stared at Gran, and then she said, "But, Gran, how can you say that when you know what the sea can do?"

"*What* can it do, Geneva?" Gran asked, and her voice was harsh. "Rise up? Swallow ships? Wash away a town? Yes, it can do all that. It can take your life, your love, everything you have that you care for. So. What should *you* do? Run away from it, as your father did? Run to Springfield and hide in a closet so you don't have to hear it or see it, or even think of it? That doesn't make it go away. It's still here, doing what it pleases. So you stay and try to keep what's left to you. You wait it out. You fight it and survive it. Lots of storms have blown across this bay, blown and gone, and I'm still here. Strong as ever. I'm not afraid of it, and never was." She sat breathing hard for a moment and then she said, in a cooler voice, "You mustn't be afraid of it, either."

Jenny was silent, her grandmother's scorn for her father burning deep inside her. Gran seemed like a rock there next to her. Invincible. And unforgiving. There was something fine in her defiance, but something heartless, too. Jenny wondered if she herself could be a rock, but looking out at the water, she doubted it. The sea was full of transformations. It was very wide, and very deep. And she was very small.

"Come," said Gran at last, pulling herself up. "We'll go inside now."

In the time that remained till bedtime, as they sat in the parlor, each with her own book open in her lap, the breeze came back gradually, first in little puffs and gusts, and then in longer sweeps that whined at the corners of the house. Gran looked up, listened, and laid her book aside. "Geneva," she said, "we've left the oilskin out on the bench. I can hear it flapping. Go out and get it, child, before it blows away."

"Yes, Gran," said Jenny. She went outside and stood in front of the house for a moment. It was growing dark very rapidly, and the sea, though it had been lying far out before, was rising, in those long, smooth swells, at a pace that seemed unusual even to Jenny's inexperienced eye. She hurried to the bench and took up the oilskin, and then, turning, she stopped short and gasped. Seward was standing on the grass between her and the house.

"Good evening, miss," he said.

"G-good evening," Jenny stammered.

"I said I'd come again," he reminded her. "I didn't mean to startle you."

Jenny stared at him, not knowing what to say.

Gran had told her she mustn't let him into the house, but what if he insisted?

"Tell her for me," he said, as if he could read her thought, "that she must give it back at once."

"She won't, though," Jenny blurted, forgetting that she was to tell him nothing. "She said so."

"She must," said Seward. "It's valued. The ship can't find its way along the bottom without its eyes. Explain to her. She must give it back now, before it's too late."

Jenny's breath caught. "Oh, please," she begged, "what do you mean? What will happen?"

"If she doesn't give it back," said Seward in that voice without emotion, "the sea will come and take it." He turned away. "Tell her," he said over his shoulder, and then he disappeared into the dark.

But, inside, Gran set her jaw and said, "Never. No matter what. Does he think I waited half a lifetime just to give up now? Don't be afraid, Geneva. Go to bed." She sat up straight in her chair, her eyes bright and hard, gripping the crutch across her knees like a weapon. "I shall stay down here tonight," she said, "and wait."

All night the hurricane—for there was a hurricane—
wheeled slowly north. Its eye rode far offshore, but
its sweeping arms of wind and rain clawed at the
nearest beaches, and the sea rose up before it in great,
spreading welts that raced for miles ahead, rolling in
to land in the measured waves Jenny had seen at
evening.

It had begun a week before, this hurricane, on the
very day of the arrival of the sign, begun as a petu-
lance deep in the Caribbean. But as it swung in an
upward arc to the west and north, its indignation
grew, the speed of its winds increased, until at last,
arriving in mid-coastal waters, it had spun itself into a
rage. It was small, no more than forty miles across, but
deadly: round its eye the winds were whirling ninety

miles an hour. It paused at dawn and hung for an hour, and then, as if its orders had been heard, its target sighted, it veered abruptly westward toward the coast, and the sea ran on ahead in a frenzy of excitement.

All night Jenny had slept in fits and starts, aware of the booming rhythm of the waves. Then, after hours of tossing, she was brought bolt upright by a sudden Niagara of rain. At the same moment a blast of wind slammed at the house, a wind that did not pass off but kept on coming, its voice rising steadily. The light was so dim that she could barely see, and could not guess what time it was. Alarmed, she slipped out of bed, pulled on her clothes, and crept downstairs, holding tight to the banister. The clock in the lower hall said eight o'clock. Morning! But it seemed more like the onset of the night.

She peered into the parlor and saw that Gran was sitting rigid in her chair, wide awake, still gripping the crutch across her knees. "Gran," Jenny quavered, "is this it? Has the hurricane come?"

"Yes," said Gran. "It's here. It's just beginning."

"Oh, Gran, what shall we do?" wailed Jenny.

"We shall wait!" Gran rapped out. "It's only a storm. Only a storm, Geneva! We shall sit here and wait it out."

Jenny was drawn almost against her will to the window, and what she saw there dizzied her. Under the darkened sky, the sea was white, running sidewise, exploding in sheets of spray against the long arm of land that formed their end of the little bay. Clots of foam fled by through the air like rushing phantoms, and the water was so high that the beach had vanished. Rain was flung past the window horizontally, so that it was hard to tell the place where it ended and the sea began. Everything was water. And noise. For the voice of the wind kept rising steadily. Jenny shrank back from the window. "Oh, Gran!" she whispered.

"It's only a storm, I tell you," Gran insisted. Her face was stony. "Go put the kettle on for tea."

Jenny went to the kitchen and took up the kettle. She was trembling so much that it rattled in her hand, and she could not get the pump to work. She leaned against the metal sink and worked the handle up and down, up and down, but nothing came. Helplessly, she went back to the parlor. "There's no water!" she exclaimed.

Gran laughed at this, a harsh, unnatural laugh. "No water!" she echoed. "Milk, then. And bread. We must keep up our strength."

They sat in the parlor with their bread and milk, but Jenny could scarcely swallow. She wanted to cover her ears, to run away, but there was nowhere to run. That other world she had accepted, that world that lay beyond the edges of the sea, had loomed up now and was blotting out, shouldering out, drowning out the real world altogether. The parlor, the house, and everything in it seemed altered—thin and un-familiar—as if the order she depended on had warped and might collapse at any moment. She wanted to cry, but Gran's fierce expression kept her from it. Her grandmother sat with narrowed eyes and ate slowly, refusing to acknowledge the rising bellow of the wind, ignoring the spray dashed in around the windows, down the complaining chimney, under the bolted door. The house trembled, Jenny trembled, the whole world trembled. Gran alone was firm.

Outside, the wind increased. Impossible, and yet its voice grew stronger, till the roaring was almost in-tolerable. Jenny doubled over on the sofa, her arms around her head, but still she dared not cry. And then, after a time, Gran seemed to notice her and said,

"Geneva. Sit up." Her voice was steely. "Take away the plates and glasses. Now."

Jenny got to her feet somehow, and did as she was told. "I *won't* cry," she told herself over and over. "I won't let her see me cry."

When she came back to the parlor, Gran said to her, "Bring me the head." Without a word, Jenny took the key from the china teapot, opened the drawer in the dining room, lifted out the wooden head, brought it to Gran. Gran took it and settled it in her lap, pushing the crutch off onto the floor. "Now," she said, "go and sit down. And wait."

Perched again on the sofa, Jenny wrung her hands and fought back tears. There was nothing else to do but sit and wait, while the storm shrieked on, all around the house. Outside, the sea rose higher and came searching almost to the top of the little bluff. Sit and wait—it can't go on forever—there isn't that much wind and water in the world. Jenny's thoughts presented these alternatives to nightmare, but other thoughts rejected them: sit and wait for the sea to come and take us—take the wooden head and me and Gran and everything.

And then, after a screaming eternity, the clock in the hall began to strike, a faint, feeble sound against the wind—bong, bong, bong, all the way up to ten. And as if the tenth stroke were a signal, the storm stopped. Suddenly. The rain stopped, the wind stopped, the room was full of dazzling sunlight. Jenny thought, "We're dead. We've gone to heaven." Her ears rang with the silence. She looked at Gran, but her grandmother sat as stiffly upright as before. "Gran!" she cried. "Is it over? How can it be over all at once like that?"

"It's *half* over," said Gran. "We're in the eye. It will only last a few minutes." She did not take her hands from the wooden head in her lap. She did not stir at all.

Jenny got up from the sofa and ventured again to the window. The sea had risen just over the top of the bluff and now, instead of rushing sidewise to the arm of land beside them, it raged like boiling water in a great pot, tumbling, churning, rushing in every direction at once, smashing against itself and casting up bursts of glittering spray. The sky overhead was a brilliant blue, with only a few loose clouds to mottle it.

But Jenny saw with horror that before them and encircling them was a towering wall of thick, black clouds, closing them in, rising from the water like the sides of a chasm, miles into the air—a chasm from which there could be no escape. She could see the top-most edges of the wall, folded back smoothly against the sky. And she could see that it was moving, its far arc gliding toward them across the furious sea.

Gran did not get up to look. She stayed where she was, her hands on the wooden head, and she said, "It will start again soon."

Jenny stood hypnotized at the window, watching as the wall of black came onward. Gradually, the room grew dimmer, the dazzling patch of sky was curtained out. And then the clouds engulfed them. Instantly, the wind began again, shrieking louder than ever, and the world outside was lost in new sheets of rain that swept in the opposite direction now, north-ward toward the town at the other end of the bay.

This shift seemed to catch the house off-guard. There was a crash high over their heads, and a sluice of water spread into the parlor from the fireplace, like blood streaming from a wound. "Why, the chimney's gone!" Gran exclaimed. She sounded shocked, sur-prised. The sudden breaching of her fortress seemed to jar her own determination; she bent a little in her chair, gripping the wooden head, and her voice had lost a fraction of its metal.

Jenny sensed the loss and it chilled her, for she had

been drawing her own slim courage from Gran. She moved backward from the window and stood distracted in the middle of the room, her hands tight over her ears now to cut the screeching wind. She had no notion what to do. Her mind was numb, her bones like jelly, and it seemed as if only the locking of her muscles could hold her upright. From the kitchen came another crash, a sound of shattering glass, and at once the house was full of wind. A lamp toppled, the curtains rose up like banners. And with a noise like a cork popping from a bottle the front door burst its bolt and was flung wide open. It hung flapping from one twisted hinge, and in the next moment the sea came over the sill.

It purled into the parlor silently, a foam-flecked, spreading puddle, soaking the braided rug, reaching across the floor. It looked harmless, a simple spill from a pitcher, easy to mop away. But Gran shrank back in her chair. She lifted the wooden head from her lap and held it close in her arms while the water rippled toward her. A low wave rushed at the doorsill and the puddle deepened, spreading rapidly, sliding around her feet, and Jenny's feet, until an inch stood on the floor, from wall to wall, and still Gran sat transfixed. The wind screamed round and round the house and rushed in through the breaches in a triumph, bringing with it salty flakes of spray. The water on the floor rose slowly, with little currents of its own that beckoned backward toward the gaping doorway even while it rippled in.

Jenny could stand it no longer. "Give the head back, Gran!" she shrilled. "Give it back!" But she could hardly hear her own voice against the wind, and she began to sob, explosively, all efforts to control her tears gone flying.

Then Gran was pushing up from her chair. Her crutch had drifted out of reach, but she stood erect without it. "All *right!*" she cried, but she was not speaking to Jenny. Her face was dark, her jaw thrust out. "All *right!*" she cried again. "All *right!*" She began to wade across the room, moving firmly in spite of her bundled foot.

Jenny's sobs caught in her throat. "Gran!" she gasped. "What are you doing?"

But Gran did not hear her, did not reply. She moved forward, the drenched hem of her skirt trailing out behind her. She came to the doorway and without a pause went out into the storm.

Jenny splashed after her. At the battered door, she shouted, "Gran! Be careful! Just drop it into the water, Gran, and then come . . ." But the shout died in her throat, for all at once it was clear that Gran did not mean to come back. She was pushing forward, leaning against the wind, out toward the flooded bluff, and she showed no signs of dropping the wooden head. Her hair tore loose from its pins and twists and streamed out sidewise. "Gran!" shrieked Jenny. "Gran, no. Come back!"

But Gran could not have heard, for the wind shrieked louder, and the waves were dragging at her knees. She staggered, her arms flew out, and the head, released at last, fell free. And as it fell, the sea rose up and swallowed it. She paused. And then she found her balance once again and struggled on, nearer to the margin of the bluff. Jenny, near fainting, floundered over the doorsill. "Gran!" she shouted. "Wait!"

Then: a miracle. A hand grasped her shoulder from behind, a voice boomed out above the wind: "Jenny! Go back." It was her father—drenched, his hair wild, his jaw thrust out like Gran's. He lifted her and set her back inside the doorway. And then he plunged out into the wind and water, and seized Gran in the final instant, just as she sagged and was dropping into the sea.

Tea. Strong, hot, with lots of sugar. It warmed away the cold of Jenny's heart as the blankets wrapped around her warmed away the shivers in her legs. She sat upstairs, in Gran's room, sipping, and watched as her father ministered to his mother. He had cut away the sodden bandages and splints from her ankle, stripped away her dripping dress and petticoats, and bundled her into bed. Then he had gone downstairs, sloshed to the kitchen, coaxed water from the balky pump. He had managed somehow to kindle a fire in the stove, had boiled water in the kettle. He was amazing. And now he was spooning tea into Gran as if he were feeding a little child, except that her cup had been sharpened with brandy. She lay quietly, accepting it. She had not said a word.

The hurricane was gone. It had whirled directly over them, moved inland, and was breaking up against the hills and trees. "Just another rainstorm by now," said Jenny's father when she asked him. "Noisy and wet, but mostly harmless. You had the worst of it here."

"But, Papa," she said, "how did you know to come?"

"I sat there in the store," he told her, "and I watched the barometers go down and down and down. Finally I couldn't stand it any longer. I hitched up the buggy and I came."

Jenny held her hand over her tea and felt the rising steam turn to dew against her palm. She was thinking about her father—coming out in the storm, coming to the sea. "Papa," she asked him, "where's the buggy now? Where's the horse?"

"I haven't any idea," he said. "After a while the wind got so bad that limbs were cracking and there were twigs flying everywhere. The horse kept shying, and at last he reared and broke the traces. He ran off, and there I was, sitting like a dummy in the buggy all alone, with rain blowing in my face. So I just climbed out and came the rest of the way on foot." He seemed, himself, amazed at this, even while he told about it.

"On foot!" Jenny exclaimed. "How far?"

"I really don't know," he answered. "A few miles."

"That must have been terrible!" said Jenny, her eyes round. "When Gran went out, I thought the wind would blow her over!"

"I didn't really think about it much," he said. "All I wanted to do was come to the two of you. Why, for all I knew, the house had flooded and you might be . . . well, never mind. It didn't happen. I got here in time."

They were quiet then. He set aside Gran's spoon and teacup, and smoothed a red-gray strand of hair away from her cheek. She sighed and closed her eyes, and he murmured to Jenny, "Come, we'll let her sleep a little now."

In her bedroom, in *his* bedroom, they sat together on the edge of the bed, and he took her hand and held it. Jenny thought about the sign—the wooden head—and wondered if he'd understand when he knew.

"You've had a bad time," he said at last.

"Oh, no!" she protested. "Not until today! Before the storm, it was—fine, mostly. Papa, do you remember a woman named Isabel Cooper?"

"Hmmm," he said. "No, I don't think so. Why?"

"Well, but do you remember a man named Nicholas?"

"Yes," he said, "if you mean Nicholas Irving, the one who carved the figurehead for the *Amaryllis*. He was like a big brother to me there for a while. Why, he taught me how to swim! But that was a long time ago, Jenny. Has Gran been talking about him?"

"Yes," said Jenny. "She's talked a lot about the old days. Nicholas Irving was in love with Isabel Cooper, but she didn't like him. That's why he tried to drown himself."

"Ah!" said her father. "Yes, I remember now. A terrible thing. Isn't it amazing what people will do for love!" He paused, and his serious expression turned into a smile. "Why, some people will even go out in a buggy in the worst storm of the age!"

"And come to the sea, even if they don't like it," Jenny added wisely.

"Yes," he said. "And come to the sea."

After a moment, she asked, "Were you scared, Papa?"

He lifted her hand and moved her fingers about, as if he was amazed at how well they worked. "You know," he said, "I didn't even stop to think about it. I just . . . got into the buggy and came."

"You were brave, the way you went and rescued Gran," said Jenny admiringly. "Maybe you won't be scared ever again after this."

There was a pause, and then he said, "Maybe not."

Jenny hopped down off the bed. "Wait here, Papa," she said. "I want to show you something." She hurried into the back bedroom and returned with the little tin trumpet and the wooden cannon. "Look, Papa. Look what we found in the trunk!"

Her father took the toys and stared at them in astonishment. "Good Lord. Why, I remember these. Imagine her saving them all this time!" He sat there thinking, and then he said, "Jenny, what was Gran doing, out there in the storm like that?"

Jenny looked at him soberly. "It's hard to explain, Papa. Wait. I've got one more thing to show you." She hurried out again and went to Gran's room. Gran was dozing, her face slack against the pillow. Jenny tiptoed in, went to the highboy in the corner, and took the gold watch from the drawer where Gran had told her to put it for safekeeping. Back in her father's room, she laid it gently in his hand. "It's for you," she said. "Grandfather had it all engraved and everything. For your twenty-first birthday. But Gran forgot." Then she added quickly, "But she's very sorry. Look inside the lid, Papa. Open it."

Her father lifted the thin back carefully and stared at the engraving. "Oh!" he whispered. Then, in a steadier voice: "Jenny, how incredible! Why, it's almost like a message, isn't it? After all these years!"

Jenny drew a deep breath. "Papa," she said, "do you believe in things you can't explain?"

He looked at her, puzzled, and then he said slowly, "Yes, I guess I do. Sometimes. Here, especially."

And so she told him everything.

Later, when the story was done, Jenny leaned her head against her father's shoulder and sighed. "But, you know, Papa, she waited so long—and now she doesn't have anything."

"But she does!" said her father. "She has us, just as she always did. Maybe she'll see that, now." He picked up the little tin trumpet and blew into it. The thin bleat sounded loud in the quiet, and he put it down quickly, but it was too late. From the next room a voice called.

"George?"

They went to the door of Gran's room and saw that she was sitting up in bed. "Well, George," she said. She sounded very tired.

"Well, Mother," he returned.

"Dear boy," she said to him, "come and kiss me."

They ate their supper upstairs in Gran's room, a supper thrown together, by Jenny and her father, any old way in the ruined kitchen. But Gran had very little appetite. She sat propped up with pillows, and she kept moving her foot under the covers.

"How does it feel?" Jenny asked.

"Light without all those bandages," she said. "But whether it's mended or not, I really can't tell."

"Well," said Jenny's father, "either way, you'd better come back to Springfield, at least until we can get someone to clean up the mess downstairs."

"Is it very bad?" she asked him.

"I'm afraid so," he said. "The wind smashed the kitchen window and blew everything all around, the front door's almost off, the chimney's gone entirely. And the floor—some of the boards are bound to warp. It may take weeks to dry."

"It's been a good house," said Gran. "It just couldn't quite hold out. I couldn't hold out, either, George. We're old, this house and I."

"And yet," he said, "you can mend, both of you."

"No," said Gran. "We can be patched up, stuck back together one way or another, perhaps, but it wouldn't last for long. You've been urging me to come and stay in Springfield for years, George. I think the time has come for me to do it now."

"We've always wanted you," he said, "but only if you really wanted to come."

She shrugged. "I'm tired," she said. "I think I'll go to sleep now."

"I'll find a horse and buggy first thing in the morning," he told her, spreading up her covers. "We'll get an early start."

"All right," she said, and closed her eyes.

Jenny went up to the bed and leaned down to kiss her grandmother's cheek. "Good night, Gran," she said.

And Gran said, "Good night . . . Jenny."

In the morning, Jenny woke to soft sunshine. She climbed out of bed and crossed to the window. Below, the beach was clean and smooth, and the sea lay smiling and slopping contentedly far down the sand. Just offshore, a gull was wheeling against the bright blue sky. "Yesterday," Jenny reminded herself, "there was a hurricane!" But it was hard to remember now. Until she remembered Gran. "We're all going home today," she murmured, and in spite of the warm sunlight, she was filled with sadness.

She was pulling on her clothes when her father appeared in the doorway. "Well, lazybones," he said, "it's about time you were up. I've been to town already and brought back a first-rate horse and buggy. Pack your things. We'll be leaving soon."

"How's Gran?" she asked him.

"She's ready," he said. "We've both had breakfast. There's milk and bread and an orange for you downstairs. Come along. I'm anxious to get started. Your mother will be worried to death."

"I'll be ready in a minute," she said.

Downstairs, it would have been impossible to forget the storm. The parlor had a dismal look and a damp, unnatural smell. Water stood in the corners, and there was wet sand crusted everywhere. From the blown-in kitchen window a light breeze stirred the limp curtains and passed on out through the space where the front door had been propped against a side of the gaping doorframe. The clock in the hall had stopped. Jenny took up her orange and, peeling it as she went, wandered sadly through the rooms. The life had gone from the house. It looked defeated.

She paused in the dining room and, sucking her orange, looked at the picture of the ship. It hung a little crooked now, but here, at least, there was spirit still. The ship was so beautiful, a crisp, strong, winged thing, the figurehead intact and calm, with the big red blossom cradled in its hands. It had a presence, an unshakable intent; it seemed almost, this morning, to leap from the frame and sail into the room. Jenny could feel its force. She lowered the orange from her mouth and stood puzzled, staring.

"Jenny!" her father called. "We're ready. Come along."

She backed away from the picture reluctantly and, turning, went through the parlor to the door. Her father was carrying Gran in his arms, crossing the strip of grass to the rented buggy. Gran's face was quiet, closed. The horse stood waiting, jingling his harness. Jenny went out across the doorsill and hesitated for a moment. The air was warm and soft and the sea sparkled, tossing up tiny whitecaps. It was very still, and yet—somewhere there was an urgency. "Just a minute," Jenny said to her father. She felt drawn strongly to the beach. She ran down across the sand, down to the water's edge, and looked out.

The flashes of sunlight reflected from the sea were blinding. She rubbed her eyes to free them of the dancing red spots that filled them and made them water. And then she began to walk along the edges of the low, ruffling waves, down the empty beach in a final tracing of the searches of the week before, still responding to the urgency that seemed to be drawing her.

Coming at last to the scrub-pine stump, she stopped and looked out again. And caught her breath. No more than ten yards out, a small, bright object floated on the swells. No, it was only the flashing of the sun in her eyes again. But something seemed to stay beyond her blinking, something reddish-orange, a vibrant spot of color that rode forward on the water. The breeze increased and the object took on dimensions, sailing nearer and nearer, and then, with a final lift of wave, it was slipped across the foam to her feet.

It was a blossom, not made of wood, but real, with six wide, curling petals, and a long white fragile stamen arching out from its cone-shaped heart. A lily, just like the one in the picture. A big red lily from the islands—an amaryllis.

Jenny bent and lifted it up, cupping it in her hands. And then she turned. "Gran!" she cried. "Oh, *Gran*!" She ran back along the beach to the bluff and crossed, up the sand, holding the blossom out before her. "Gran!" she cried again.

As she ran, Gran rose up in the buggy—rose up and then climbed down and went to meet her, striding with long, strong steps. They came together and Gran seized the blossom. Color seemed to flood from it up into her face. And as she stood there, tears running down her cheeks, the breeze came up and whispered once more: *True to yo-o-o-ou.*

Later, as the buggy rolled away, Gran said briskly to her son, "We may have to lay a new floor, George, but that shouldn't be too difficult. And the chimney can be built back up with the same old bricks."

"I can do a lot of the work myself," he said. "We'll rest up at home for a day or two and then bring every-body back and get started. I need a vacation, anyway. Exercise. Do you know I haven't been swimming in years?"

"I know," said Gran. "You're white as a clam."

As their talk went on, Jenny sat looking backward at the battered house dropping away behind them. And then she saw a short, dark figure standing on the beach. He was looking after them, and on an impulse Jenny lifted an arm and waved. He stood motionless, and then he turned and walked away down the beach, but his step seemed lighter to her, now, than it had before. As he disappeared, the sea flashed its wide green smile and answered her wave with a careless toss of foam. She leaned far out of the buggy and shouted to it, "We're coming back!" And then she settled herself in her seat and put a hand into the pocket of her pinafore. There was sand in the pocket, and she chased it around the thready inside seam with her fingertips, humming under her breath.

The buggy topped the rise and rolled on under a stand of trees, and after a while came to a fence along the road, behind which a few cows were grazing peacefully. There was a boy at work in the grass, picking up the litter of twigs and small branches scattered by the vanished storm, and as the buggy passed him, he straightened and stared at Jenny with wide-eyed admiration. She ignored him, holding her chin high, and said to herself, "That's silly." But she retied the ribbon that held back her hair, settling its bow more carefully, and smiled all the way to Springfield.

GOFISH

What did you want to be when you grew up?
When I was a preschooler, I wanted to be a pirate, and then when I started school, I wanted to be a librarian. But in the fourth grade, I got my copy of *Alice in Wonderland / Alice Through the Looking-Glass* and decided once and for all that I wanted to be an illustrator of stories for children.

When did you realize you wanted to be a writer?
I didn't even think about writing. My husband wrote the story for the first book. But then he didn't want to do it anymore, so I had to start writing my own stories. After

130

all, you can't make pictures for stories unless you have stories to make pictures for.

What's your first childhood memory?
I have a lot of preschool memories, all from when we lived in a little town just south of Columbus, Ohio. I kind of remember sitting in a high chair. And when I was a little older, I remember seeing Jack Frost looking in through the kitchen window. *That* was pretty surprising.

What's your most embarrassing childhood memory?
I don't remember any. I'm probably just suppressing them all.

What's your favorite childhood memory?
I think I liked best the times when my sister and I would curl up next to our mother while she read aloud to us.

As a young person, who did you look up to most?
No question: my mother.

What was your worst subject in school?
Arithmetic. I think you call it math now.

What was your best subject in school?
Art. And after that, English.

What was your first job?
It was when I was a teenager. I worked in what we called the College Shop in a big downtown Cleveland (Ohio) department store called Higbee's. But after that, I mostly worked in the pricing department of a washing machine factory.

How did you celebrate publishing your first book?
I don't think I did anything special. By that time, I was beginning to get over my absolute astonishment at having found my editor in the *first* place. That was the most wonderful moment of all.

Where do you write your books?
I think about them for a long time before I actually start putting words on paper, and I think about them all over the place. Then, when I'm ready, I work at my computer in my workroom. But before, I always wrote them out longhand, sitting on my sofa in the living room. I wrote on a big tablet, and then I typed everything, paragraph by paragraph, on my typewriter, making changes as I went along.

Where do you find inspiration for your writing?
I mostly write about all the unanswered questions I still have from when I was in elementary school.

132

Which of your characters is most like you?
The main characters in all of my long stories are like me, but I think Winnie Foster, in *Tuck Everlasting,* is most like me.

When you finish a book, who reads it first?
Always my editor, Michael di Capua. His opinion is the most important one.

Are you a morning person or a night owl?
Neither one, really. I'm mostly a middle-of-the-day person.

What's your idea of the best meal ever?
One that someone else cooked. And it has to have something chocolate for dessert.

Which do you like better: cats or dogs?
Cats to look at and to watch, but dogs to own.

What do you value most in your friends?
Good talk and plenty of laughing.

Where do you go for peace and quiet?
Now that my children are grown and gone into lives of their own, I have plenty of peace and quiet just sitting around the house.

SQUARE FISH

What makes you laugh out loud?
Words. My father was very funny with words, and I grew up laughing at the things he said.

What's your favorite song?
Too many to mention, but most of them are from the '30s and '40s, when songs were to *sing*, not to shout and wiggle to.

Who is your favorite fictional character?
No question: Alice from *Alice in Wonderland* and *Alice Through the Looking-Glass.*

What are you most afraid of?
I have a fear that is very common when we are little, and I seem to have hung on to it: the fear of being abandoned.

What time of year do you like best?
May is my favorite month.

What is your favorite TV show?
I don't watch many shows anymore—just CNN News and old movies.

If you were stranded on a desert island, who would you want for company?
My husband, Sam.

If you could travel in time, where would you go?
Back to Middletown, Ohio, to Lincoln School on Central Avenue, to live through fifth grade again. And again and again.

What's the best advice you have ever received about writing?
No one single thing. Too many good things to list.

What do you want readers to remember about your books?
The questions without answers.

What would you do if you ever stopped writing?
Spend all my time doing word puzzles and games, and practicing the good old songs on my piano.

What do you like best about yourself?
That I can draw, and play the good old songs on my piano.

What is your worst habit?
Always expecting things to be perfect.

What is your best habit?
Trying to make things as perfect as I can.

What do you consider to be your greatest accomplishment?
Right now, it's a picture for a new book that hasn't even been published yet. It's a picture of a man in a washtub, floating on the ocean in a rainstorm. I'm really proud of that picture.

Where in the world do you feel most at home?
That's a hard question. My family moved away from Middletown, Ohio (see the question/answer about time travel), when I was in the middle of sixth grade, and we never went back. Even after all these years, though, Middletown is the place I think of when I think about "home." I've lived in a lot of different places, though, and liked them all, so I don't feel sorry for myself. It's just that the word "home" has its own kind of special meaning.

What do you wish you could do better?
Everything. Cook, write, play the piano, everything.

What would your readers be most surprised to learn about you?
Maybe that I believe that writing books is a long way from being important. The most important thing anyone can do is be a teacher. As for those of us who write books, I often think we should all stop for fifty years. There are so many wonderful books to read, and not

enough time to get around to all of them. But we writers just keep cranking them out. All we can hope for is that readers will find at least a little time for them, anyway.